you can't see the
elephants

you can't see the
elephants

SUSAN KRELLER
translated by Elizabeth Gaffney

G. P. Putnam's Sons | An Imprint of Penguin Group (USA)

G. P. PUTNAM'S SONS
an imprint of Penguin Random House LLC
375 Hudson Street, New York, NY 10014

First published in the United States 2015
by G. P. Putnam's Sons Books for Young Readers
Originally published in Germany 2012
by Carlsen Verlag GmbH under the title *Elefanten sieht man nicht*
Edited and published in the English language
by arrangement with Carlsen Verlag GmbH
Text copyright © 2015 by Susan Kreller
English translation copyright © 2015 by Elizabeth Gaffney
The translation of this work was supported by a grant from the Goethe-Institut
(Goethe-Institut ◑▬) which is funded by the German Ministry of Foreign Affairs.

Library of Congress Cataloging-in-Publication Data
is available upon request.

Printed in the United States of America.
ISBN 978-0-399-17209-0
1 3 5 7 9 10 8 6 4 2

Design by Ryan Thomann.
Text set in Berling.

To all the others
—S.K.

THE ELEPHANT IN THE ROOM—a topic that everyone knows about but which, out of fear or a sense of discomfort, no one will discuss.

1

What happened in the blue house brought me a lot of dirty looks. It also brought me my father. The looks continued till the end of summer, but my father went away again after only two hours. I really would have liked it if he stayed a little longer. Maybe at some point he would have told me that what I'd done wasn't wrong after all, or just slightly wrong, almost right. But all that he thought, there in my grandparents' garden, was to ask if I couldn't have done things a little differently.

Meanwhile, my grandmother was stirring her coffee cold and my grandfather was anxiously reading the *Clinton Weekly*. On the back page were the words *Cool Waters Tempt Young and Old* and *Alfred Esser Appointed Chief of Fire Department*. If you looked closely, you could see that my grandfather was trembling. The headlines quivered like birch leaves in a high wind, only there was no wind that afternoon. The sun beat down on the garden chairs, and there was nothing in the sky but two or three jet trails, small flaws in the ceiling of that glowing hot day.

After stirring fifty-odd times, till we didn't think she could stir anymore, my grandmother finally stopped moving her spoon and said with a tortured expression that she could never go back to her exercise class because the others would talk. Siggy would talk, Trudy, even Hilda, who had always given her a ride to class. But she wasn't responsible for her granddaughter's behavior, was she? Grandpa lowered his newspaper, and my father growled something that began with *thirteen* and ended with *old enough*. I would have liked to have grumbled something back at him, but all I said was, "How long are you going to stay?"

2

Go play with the others."

"Grandma, they won't talk to me."

"Not even Robert Bauer?"

"Won't talk to me."

"They won't say anything?"

"They won't say a thing. I end up just standing there. Can I go now?"

"Even Robert?"

"Uh-huh."

"And the rest of them? The ones who used to meet by the old tree? What was it, a maple?"

"Grandma!"

"Them too? Well then, go see Trudy. She'll be glad to see you."

"She's almost seventy. What am I supposed to do with her? And it was a sycamore tree."

"Then go to the pool."

"I'm not going to the pool. Everyone stares at me when I go by myself."

"Then go see Trudy. She won't stare."

"Maybe because she's half-blind."

"Mascha!"

"Grandma!"

Clinton was the most boring town in the world. I may not have seen many towns in my life, but I'm still sure of that. It was truest in the neighborhood where my grandparents lived, the place where I'd spent all my summer vacations ever since my mother had died, seven years ago. It was a subdivision where all the paths that led to the redbrick houses curved in an orderly fashion, without either weeds or people. If you were from the city, like I was, you sometimes had the feeling that a train had just pulled away in front of you and left you standing all alone on the platform. The only time you saw people was when they washed their cars or went to their golf clubs or took care of the hydrangeas in their silent front yards.

"Hi Mascha!" they would say.

Or "How's school?"

They were as old as they were scarce, these people. They wore tinted glasses and had white hairs on their arms, and had no kids. The few families that did have kids had either lived here forever or had just moved here in the past few years and didn't really count. At least that's the way it sounded when my grandmother gossiped about them with her friends. The other ones did count though. The ones who had always lived here. It was just that since you never saw them on the street, they counted very quietly.

It was so quiet that the silence pounded in my ears, though sometimes there would be someone mowing the grass, back and forth and back and forth, keeping it short and tidy, but never on Sundays. And there I stood, surrounded by all this lawn-mower silence, with nothing to do and all the time in the world.

At the beginning, I liked going to my grandparents'. I liked the playground and my little bike rides and even the cookouts with the neighbors and the dry crackers they sold at the public pool.

Of course I could have spent my time reading and keeping in touch with my friends back home, but sometimes you just can't. The letters begin to blur, and then you stare at a fly on the wall or the useless clock in the kitchen that can't even be bothered to move its hands.

There was simply no one there who I could do anything with. The old ones were too old, the young too young, and everyone in between—the ones who were my age—didn't want anything to do with me. There wasn't any real reason for it, was there? When the few kids who were my age met up by the old sycamore tree or in front of the supermarket, they didn't send me away but they didn't pay me any attention either. It was just that I wasn't one of them. I was an even lower form of life than someone who had recently moved there. I was invisible. They knew I would only be there for the summer. And what I was doing there, no one knew for certain, especially me.

Even so, I was outside all the time, because inside, at my grandparents', there was nothing, nothing at all, not even a grain of dust. When I was outside, I was always in one of two places: either the blue house—but more about that later—or the playground at the edge of the neighborhood. It was mostly sand, tons of sand, with a few swings, a seesaw and a carousel. Whenever I was at the playground—and I was almost always there—I sat with my earbuds and music player on top of a little wooden fort and listened to music while four-year-olds wobbled across a hanging bridge to a slide, avoiding me.

There were definitely more exciting things in life, but there was nothing really terrible about it. From the wooden fort, you could watch the mothers squinting their mother-squints whenever their kids used sand toys that didn't belong to them. You could see the parents smoking and talking on their cell phones while their kids quietly stuffed sand in their mouths. The only reason their children didn't fall off the fort was because I made a point of sitting on the high spot, which had a roof but no railings. It wasn't much of a playground, but it was something. You couldn't expect much more from that neighborhood.

Of course I was too old for the playground. I was three times the age of kids it was meant for. My grandmother was embarrassed that I went there so often. To be seen at a playground at the age of thirteen was an obvious failure. *Mascha! At your age!* But that's the way it was. At just that age, I sat there, watched the hours creep across the sand. It was there that on the first Sunday of vacation, shortly before lunch, I met Julia and Max.

3

Julia and Max Brandner were the only people under seventy in the entire neighborhood who would talk to me. Though they took their time doing it and in the end, didn't say much. But back at the beginning, they weren't Julia and Max yet. They were just the girl and the boy. You couldn't tell anything more about them.

The day the girl in the yellow shirt first showed up at the playground, the weather kept changing, like it couldn't make up its mind. I was sitting at the top of the fort and had a roof over my head, so either way was fine with me. The rain fell straight past me, and the sunshine couldn't get in.

At first, I hardly noticed them. I had already forgotten about the yellow spot of girl that moved slowly across the sand, followed by a second, sniffling, thicker spot, almost before I even saw them. All I saw was the rain, which was bright and smelled like sand and asphalt and the wrong town. I probably wouldn't ever have noticed

8

them, but then, while the boy sat on the carousel and spun wildly through the pouring rain, the girl climbed up to my fort. She sat beside me, but I pretended I didn't see her. I turned up my music and concentrated on the rain and the boy on the carousel, who had gotten completely soaked and now began to throw a small temper tantrum. He was very fat. His stomach drooped in two equal rings over the waist of his sopping-wet pants. I pictured how he would look in a class photo: grim, as if the weight of the world were on his shoulders.

The girl was staring at me. I saw this from the corner of my eye, and I didn't like it. I could feel her eyes on my skin. The rain continued to fall. I could hear the drops through my music. Maybe it was the rain that made me so restless, but suddenly I took out my earbuds, turned to the girl and looked her straight in the face.

That face.

It was very pretty, and my first feeling was envy, envy of such a pretty face. I imagined that face at school, happily surrounded by other faces, friends everywhere, playing together at recess, getting valentines. I imagined how well-liked, how not-invisible that face must be at school. The girl had long brown hair and green eyes with golden flecks. She had no more than five freckles on her nose, and the nose beneath the freckles was small with an upturned tip. Surely, I thought, that nose must delight its parents and its relatives, its friends and the authors of its love notes.

No one had ever been delighted by my nose. You could have used a thousand words to describe it, or you could just say that it was large and hooked.

Hooked nose, garden hose!

Mascha, freak, toucan's beak!

On some people, a nose like mine may not have stood out, but on me, it did. First of all because I was short. I also had freckles—and more than just five, a lot more. My skin was more freckles than not. When you added it all together, the nose and being short and the freckles, I wasn't going to win any beauty contests. At least that's what my grandmother always said.

"Awful rain, huh?"

—

"I've never seen you here before. Is that your brother over there?"

—

"Did you just move here? You weren't here last summer."

—

"Argh!"

—

"What, don't you talk?"

—

"Look, see that boy over there that's fighting with the

rain? Who looks like he wants to beat up the rain? Is he your brother or not?"

And then, as if the rain, too, was fed up with that wild downpour, poof, it just stopped. The kids weren't ready for such a sudden change, especially not the boy, who grasped on to the carousel afraid and sat there motion-less, as if he would dry off more quickly if he didn't move.

And the strange yellow girl with the pretty face who had been sitting there the whole time with just a small corner of the fort's roof over her head suddenly realized something that I had noticed a long time ago: the left side of her shirt was soaked. The damp yellow material looked green and tired. She lifted up the sweater and began to desperately squeeze out the wet part. I glanced over at the fat boy. He was talking to two other kids, who had appeared out of nowhere. But really, he wasn't talking to them—he was staring at the ground.

"Baby elephant!" they shouted. "Baby elephant!"

In the meantime, the girl's shirt just wouldn't dry, so she yanked it over her head, accidentally pulling up the undershirt she wore beneath it. For a couple of seconds, her belly showed. It was just chance that I happened to look back at her at that exact moment. It was really just the blink of an eye. Then she pulled her shirt back down, making the giant purple-brown, yellow-rimmed marks on her belly disappear.

4

There are more ways in the world to get bruises than there are types of chocolate or television shows, and if you bothered to write down each of them, it wouldn't make the bruises go away. You can get bruises while riding your bike if you whack your leg on the pedal. You can get them in the cafeteria if someone who wants their lunch first shoves you out of the way. You get them in winter when you fall down ice-skating, and even in the night when you bang your hip into the kitchen counter on your way to the fridge in the dark. Actually, there's not a single moment in life when these marks aren't lurking, blue and green, yellow and brown, around the very next corner.

What I couldn't imagine, after I first met the girl at the playground, was how these giant bruises could have landed directly on her stomach, when they clearly belonged on other parts of her body. Maybe the girl had leapt from the high dive at the pool and not seen that there was a kickboard floating directly beneath her. Or maybe she had been lying down under an apple tree and a bunch of apples fell on her stomach, though to be honest I had never heard of such a thing happening.

I wasn't satisfied with the kickboard or the apples. There was something else the girl was hiding beneath her shirt, and even if I didn't know exactly what it was, I sensed it was nothing good.

But know? No, I couldn't know.

I waited for the kids to come back to the playground.

Four long days I waited.

When I saw them again, the boy and the girl, it was just like the first time: the girl sat silently on the wooden fort, and the boy spun madly on the carousel. *Seen that, done that*, next. But this time, it wasn't raining.

After a while, the fat boy jumped off the carousel and trudged over to the fort. When he came over, he just stood there, and if you think they finally said something, that boy and that girl, then you would be wrong.

Again the kids made fun of him.

"Hey, fatso!"

"So, how much do elephants eat?"

They weren't very imaginative. The kids couldn't think of anything worse to call him than *elephant*. The boy did flinch while trying to scrape a hole in the side of the fort with his fingernail.

What do you do when you see someone being bullied? Dad told me that he was once on a bus when a woman was being harassed by a couple of teenagers. The woman was just sitting there all by herself, and she had a big red birthmark on her face. The whole left side was red, and these kids came up with at least twenty insults to describe it. At some point my father couldn't stand it anymore. He got up from his seat and sat down next to the strange woman and said, "Oh, hello, how are you? So funny to run into you here of all places." The kids laid off her, but the woman wasn't grateful for what my father had done.

"Leave me alone!" she shouted at him.

Dad came home in a rage that evening, and a little sadder than usual, too.

"Mascha," he said to me. "Let me tell you, it's better not to help anyone. They don't want it."

It was pretty strange for him to talk that way, since he was a documentary filmmaker, and the films he made were primarily about people who rescued other people.

As for the boy at the playground, no one helped him. After all those insults, he had tears streaming from his eyes. Being silent wasn't working out so well for him. That was the first time I heard the girl's voice. I was shocked, really. I hadn't expected it, but suddenly, there she was, sitting beside me, yelling at the boys.

"Don't you talk to him about elephants!"

5

W hat's the deal with the elephants?" I ask.

"Well, what do you think? I've tried to talk to him about it."

"What did you tell him? He's your brother, right?"

"That's Max. He's seven. And yeah, he's my brother."

"Oh, okay. So what did you tell him?"

"I was trying to tell him how great elephants are and that he doesn't have to cry when those boys say that, because elephants are really smart."

"That's great."

"No, it's not. I also told him that elephants know when they're going to die. The ones in Africa know. I saw it on TV. They go off to a swamp and wait awhile, and eventually, they die."

And then the girl told me how her brother had tried to do it. Die, I mean. He'd stuffed about a thousand chocolate bars in his pockets, tucked a wool blanket under his arm and then, as quietly as an elephant—because elephants are actually very quiet, if I could imagine that, crept down to the rec room in the basement. There in the rec room, he sat down on the sofa and laid out the chocolate bars on the floor beside him, just in case he was too hungry to die, and then he waited, waited for death. Two hours later, she had found him there. His death was delayed, since his sister happened to get there first, and so Max had been forced to live on—with a thousand chocolate bars in his belly.

"Can you imagine, Mama and Daddy didn't even notice that Max had gone off to die. Daddy, well—"

"What did he do?"

"He cussed him out and told him he shouldn't eat so much. The candy wrappers were everywhere."

"Huh."

I couldn't think of anything more clever to say. I had never had a conversation like this before. The closest was with my father, who sometimes talked about death. It was pretty normal for him, ever since my mom died, but it sounded really weird coming from Julia. There was too much death and definitely too much about elephants. It wouldn't have felt right to talk to her about some new actor or cool brand of cell phone either, though. It just wouldn't have worked, even if I knew anything about either actors or cell phones. My phone was old. I'd inherited it from my father. At school, kids sometimes asked me why I'd brought my landline to school.

My music player was the most up-to-date device that I had, and it wasn't because we didn't have money. It was because my father didn't know anything about what was expected of a thirteen-year-old at school.

Max was now standing at the base of the wooden fort, looking up at us with red-rimmed eyes. He didn't seem to know what to do with his hands. He was running one of them through his hair, which was dark brown and long for a boy, especially in front. As he pushed his bangs aside, I saw two things:

The first was that Max's eyes were just as beautiful as his sister's, green with gold. The other was another story, not green and certainly not gold, but red and purple. It was a cut about the size of a nickel on the right side of his forehead. I hadn't seen many cuts in my life, but this one looked bad enough that I wanted to ask Max, *What did you do to yourself?* Even if there were definitely better questions to ask. Unfortunately, I didn't get the chance, because before I was able to open my mouth, the girl beside me said, "I'm Julia!" Then she jumped down off the fort, grabbed her brother by the hand and ran off with him.

6

It wasn't the elephants that got me talking with Julia the next time, it was my father's music. Even so, the subject was awkward. My father wasn't into the music you'd hear on the radio.

"What kind of music do you listen to, anyway?" she asked.

"I told you when I came, I was a stranger. I told you when I came, I was a stranger."

"What?" she asked. "Are you crazy?"

"It's Leonard Cohen. That's what I'm listening to. Do you know him?"

"Nope, never heard of him."

"Well, those are the lyrics to 'The Stranger Song.' It's my favorite," I said.

"Huh. Can I listen?"

Since Dad explained the lyrics to me, I always knew what the songs were about, no matter how complicated it all sounded. I loved those lyrics. Leonard Cohen sang about blue raincoats and women in feathers and then about birds with their own feathers sitting on wires and somehow making the best of it all. What I liked most was that during the conversations we had about Leonard Cohen's lyrics my father actually talked to me for once. We'd sit at the kitchen table, letting our hands stick to the plastic tablecloth, and listen to an old CD. Now and then my father would lift his index finger and smile. *Listen to that, listen carefully, Mascha.* In those moments, I swear, everything was as good as it possibly could have been.

When my father talked about Leonard Cohen, it always sounded like they were old friends, but the truth was my father had never been to one of his concerts, not even once. He was going to have to hurry if he wanted to catch his feathered friend while he was still alive, because Leonard Cohen was getting old. His voice was getting deeper as he aged.

Dad had a deep voice, too, though he wasn't that old. Since he hardly ever used his deep voice to talk to me, I had sort of borrowed Leonard Cohen's voice for him in my mind, and whenever I put in the earbuds and listened, Dad was there. At the moment, however, my father was playing in Julia's ears.

After a while, she said, "I like it. Hey, what's your name, anyway?"

"Mascha. So, do you really like it?"

"Sure. It's beautiful."

"The kids in my class listen to other stuff. I wouldn't play this for them. Can you imagine, Leonard Cohen is over eighty."

"Doesn't sound like it."

"Well, because he was much younger when he sang this song. A lot younger, actually."

"Oh, I get it. I don't listen to anything at home. I'm not allowed to bother Daddy with any kind of music."

"Why not?"

"He has so much stress at work. He doesn't need more at home."

"Music isn't stressful!"

"For him it is."

That was when I first realized that Max wasn't at the playground. I had gotten used to him always being there with her. Even if you didn't see him, he was always standing somewhere off at the edges.

"Hey, that's weird, where's your brother?"

She answered me loudly and suddenly.

"He fell down!"

"Fell down? How?"

"I don't know. Down some flight of stairs."

"Was it bad?"

"No."

"Huh."

"Huh."

"Those boys are so mean to him."

"There's nothing I can do. They don't listen to me anyway. They just keep doing it."

"It's terrible."

"Yeah, I guess so. Max doesn't have any friends in his class. No one will sit next to him. No one will do anything with him. They all say he stinks."

"Do they hit him?"

"No, they don't beat him up. It's kind of weird, but none of them ever hit him. His whole class just acts like he has cooties. If someone touches him by accident, they all scream *Ewwww!* But I don't know, mostly they just talk. And they like to call him baby elephant, like you heard."

"Yeah, I heard."

"Max gets that all the time."

Julia and I went on talking, but not about Max. We sat on the wooden fort, kicked up our legs and watched the sand castles growing taller and being demolished. We told each other our last names and where we lived. Julia's name was Brandner, and she lived in a big bluish-red house that I had walked past a thousand times that wasn't far from my grandparents'. She was nine.

Now and then, I would play Julia a song that made her close her eyes and say, "That's beautiful." And it seemed to me that a few good things had come together: a sunny day and a playground and a girl who lived nearby and said repeatedly, *That's beautiful.* Later, when we said good-bye, Julia looked happier than she had before. When she'd walked a little ways off, she turned back and called out to me across the playground.

"Mascha!"

"Yeah?"

"I do watch out for him, you know!"

7

didn't see Julia and Max for a week after that. At first it was my fault, or really my grandparents', because they had so much celebrating to do. Summer in Clinton meant that I had to endure three birthday parties in a single week of July, and they all stank of perfume, coffee and wine. First was my grandfather's birthday, and then my grandmother's, and then on Saturday, they celebrated both together. Each time, I kid you not, half the neighborhood came over. On the actual birthdays, they just dropped in, but for the party they showed up with their shirts and skirts neatly ironed.

I think my grandparents were well liked in the neighborhood. At least they were on their birthdays. It wasn't that hard to be liked there, to belong. All you had to do was mow your grass, buy tulips at the farmers' market, bring a few tidbits of gossip to choir practice, always have lived there, vote for the king and queen of the local Mardi

Gras festival and celebrate approximately one couple's golden anniversary each week. But you really had to do it all. My grandparents did. They shared the duties for the most part, except for the fact that Grandpa preferred to take care of the chores that didn't require as much conversation.

I always had to chat with people at the parties. *How do you do, yes, hello, no, the vacation has just begun, yes, I've gotten older, I've grown, well, better to grow than not to.* At the third party, I was spitting out all the usual answers, until Trudy, who lived in the house diagonally across the street, asked me with her cigarette breath, "So, are you still such a loner, Mascha?"

Finally I was able to give a new answer.

"No, I know someone here now. I met two kids. At the playground."

"Oh really? Then you've had luck."

"Yep. The Brandner kids. Do you know them?"

"Oh, I see."

"Does that mean you know them?"

"I don't know if I *know* them. The way one knows people. Won't you come by and visit me sometime? I have some new rabbits. I just got them yesterday. Just come by, anytime. You'll like them. You used to like feeding my rabbits."

"Okay. So, do you know their parents?"

"Which parents?"

"Julia and Max's."

"Oh, yes, right. Julia and Max. Yes, dear, of course I do. Very nice people. Do you know the car dealership?"

"Sure."

"Well, you see, the Brandners own the dealership. Joe got his car there."

Then Trudy was gone, and then the others were gone, too, and then it was night, and then it was day, and I went back to the playground. I didn't see Julia and Max. And I kept not seeing them. At first it didn't bother me—I just felt a little lonely and would have liked to have them there, so that I wasn't so alone. But as time passed, I began to worry. I don't know why, because I really didn't know a thing about them, then.

On the eighth day, I set out to look for them. I knew where the Brandners lived, even if I'd never rung the bell. I just wanted to see if Julia and Max would come to the playground with me, or wherever—it didn't matter where. It was just a couple of blocks: I walked along the street, turned left, went straight, crossed another narrow street and there I was, in front of the Brandners' beautiful bluish-red house, which seemed bigger to me than it ever had before.

The front yard was more orderly than my grandparents', if that was even possible. The flower beds were raked and free of weeds, and everywhere grew bright blue hydrangeas. Everybody in the neighborhood loved hydrangeas. Those neatly trimmed, ball-shaped bushes seemed to lurk around every corner.

I stood there and suddenly felt guilty, which was ridiculous. There was no reason for it. Maybe it was just because I had passed the house so often without ever really looking at it. Maybe it was because I didn't really know Julia and Max. Still, I rang. Or I tried to. It took a long time for my index finger, which was circling the bell, finally to land on the polished golden dot.

I pressed the button.

Nothing.

I didn't hear any ringing.

Again.

Nothing.

After I'd pressed the button a couple more times and nothing had happened, I walked around the right side of the house to the garden. Maybe they were all outside and that's why they hadn't heard me. But there was no one in the garden. I was just about to go when I heard something that made me walk over to the window. It wasn't open, but I could still hear. Not words. There were words underneath the sound, but it was impossible to make them out.

What I heard was screaming.

This horrible screaming.

And when I looked through the window I saw something that was more than a glimpse of a bruised belly, or a gash on a brow. For the first time in my life, I couldn't catch my breath. The air wouldn't go into me. There was just a whistling in my throat. Breathe, I thought, breathe, but the truth was I thought nothing, I only felt. Breathe, breathe, please breathe. When my body finally heard me, and the air came back into my lungs, and I could think again, I didn't bang on the shutter or call the neighbors. When I could think again, I jumped up and ran and ran and ran. But no matter how far I ran, the screams stayed in my ears.

8

My grandmother has always said you can tell a tidy person by the corners of their room. Even if you've run your finger along the shelves and examined the windowsills in bright sunlight, you have to look in the corners. You can only tell if a person is really clean by looking in the nooks and crannies. If I had told Grandma on that July evening that the Brandners had dust in their corners, even if it were just balls of lint, she would have definitely listened. Instead, when I said, "The Brandners are going to kill their children eventually," and all she could think to reply as she dried the dishes was, "Why would you ever say such a thing?"

I said it was because the Brandners were going to kill their children eventually and because it was just an oversight that they hadn't already.

"You've gone crazy, Mascha, my goodness."

"Grandma, I'm telling you, they beat their children. I know."

"That's not possible! Do you understand me? That cannot be! Stop it. Just stop it."

"Why can't it be true? Listen."

"Mascha! The Brandners own the car dealership on the hill. You know that. They're good people. Everyone here knows that. Those things don't happen here!"

"Julia has giant blue bruises. And Max has an actual gash on his head."

"And? All children look like that. You used to look like that, too, little girl, exactly. You were always falling down. All children look like that."

"They beat their children."

"Mascha! You have no idea what you're saying. Do you know how embarrassing it would be for us if you said such a thing? If you tell anyone else?"

"Grandma, Julia has bruises on her stomach!"

"Be quiet, child! Enough! The Brandners would never do such a thing, never. They're upstanding people. Where do you think we bought our car?"

"I've seen what they do to their children. What Mr. Brandner does to them."

"How can you possibly have seen that? And what did you see anyway, a couple of slaps? It never did your father any harm."

"Maybe it did. Take a look at him."

"Mascha, what is wrong with you? Are you just trying to make trouble? Are you bored? Is that it?"

"Grandma, I saw through their window. I saw their father shove Max against a wall. I heard the screaming."

"Max is always screaming. The Brandners have always had problems with him. That's the way he is. And who knows what you were really seeing?"

"Grandma, only Mr. Brandner was screaming. Max was completely silent."

9

The silence was the worst part. Max had let himself be thrown against the wall, and his head had banged against a picture frame that looked like it was metal. He didn't even try to defend himself. Not for one second. He just let it happen to him while his father shouted something that I couldn't make out. Julia, who was standing near the couch, was staring at nothing—or everything except her brother. It was a very different stare from the one I'd seen back at the wooden fort. There was nothing in Julia's eyes. Nothing.

Not even tears.

I didn't think there were tears in Max's either, though I couldn't be certain because of his long hair. But what I had seen was worse than tears.

It took a long time before my grandmother would even come close to listening to me, at least half an hour. And once she had heard me out, she just began to explain it away. Every second sentence was about what good people the Brandners were, how capable, important and clean.

Beyond that, it was all about how the car dealership wasn't doing well and they couldn't take a summer vacation like they always had and how everything was going badly. I also heard how Mr. Brandner had always had a temper, and how his wife was the opposite, but that his father had been the same way—hot-tempered and loud—and Mr. Brandner took after his father.

She didn't want to hear the first thing about Mr. Brandner slamming his children into walls, and neither did my grandfather.

The whole time, he'd been leaning against the kitchen sink, like he was following along, but when I asked him if he had anything to say, he just grumbled. Besides mowing the grass, that was his favorite thing to do, grumbling. Sometimes he actually sounded a little like his lawn mower.

He grumbled so much, you'd think he only had bones and organs inside him, not a single thought or word. He probably would have liked to grumble constantly, but in between it was sometimes necessary for him to brush his teeth or breathe or something like that.

It wasn't true, though, that my grandfather was nothing but bones and organs. There was more to him. Every once in a while, he allowed himself some fun, which he couldn't have done if he were really empty inside. Sometimes, for example, he would pretend that he was going to break the neighborhood rule against making noise on Sundays. He would haul the lawn mower out of the shed and set it in the middle of the lawn. When my grandmother rushed outside and started to lecture him on common decency, neighbors and following the rules, he would take up a screwdriver, begin tinkering with the mower and wink at me. And in that wink were all the questions, answers and complaints, and conversations he usually avoided.

That July evening, though, he didn't wink, just shuffled out of the kitchen. Grandma also had something important to do in another room, probably some dusting. And me? I stood alone at the kitchen window. I couldn't get Julia's staring and Max's silence out of my head. I still felt the same way half an hour later—sad and small—and so I decided to do something out of the ordinary. I called my father.

10

My father and I never spoke on the telephone when I was at my grandparents'. Even when he called for their birthdays, he didn't want to talk to me, just had them pass on a message: *Oh yeah, say hi to Mascha for me.* Most of the time I didn't mind. After a couple years, I got used to him wanting a few weeks alone every year to grieve for my mother. But then sometimes I would forget I'd gotten used to it, and in those moments, I missed him.

The day she died, my mother had been sitting in the garden drinking lemonade and swatting at wasps. She had breathed and breathed, and then she stopped. She'd vanished from our lives. And ever since, during summer vacations, I left my father alone, and came here to listen to music.

But after my grandparents left me in the kitchen, I couldn't stand it anymore. I went to the guest room, which was my room in the summers when I stayed with my grandparents, and got my cell phone.

The room was so neat. It didn't seem possible for me to sit down on one of the white-painted chairs and tell my father about Julia's bruised stomach. So I got into bed, pulled the freshly washed covers over my head and made my call in the dark.

"Yes?"

"Dad, it's me."

"Is something wrong with Grandma?"

"What? No. Why do you think there's something wrong with Grandma?"

"Well, why are you calling?"

"I have to tell you something."

"All right. Tell me."

"I met these two kids at the playground. I think they're being beaten by their parents."

"Do you think it, or do you know it?"

"Um, well, they have so many bruises. And the boy has a cut on his forehead and is very odd."

"Mascha, you have to be careful. They could have been hurt some other way."

"But I've also seen it."

"What have you seen?"

"I looked through their window and saw Max being thrown against the wall by his father. He hit his head really hard."

"Huh. Did you really see this?"

"Yes."

"Mascha, this kind of thing should be taken care of by the police or Child Protective Services."

"Well how are the people from Child Protective Services supposed to know they need to deal with it?"

"Someone else will tell them. If you've seen it, someone else must have, too. The neighbors, for instance, or the teacher, or the pediatrician. Eventually, someone will say something."

"*Eventually?* Julia and Max will be dead."

"That's ridiculous, Mascha. People don't just die that quickly."

"But someone has to do something."

"Yes, but not you. You are too young. You can't do anything."

People don't just die that quickly, Dad had said. I couldn't believe he'd said it. My father knew exactly how quickly—how unbelievably quickly—a person could die. How sometimes it could happen in a single second. Suddenly, there would be fewer cups of coffee drunk or beds made. What upset me even more was that my father was usually interested in other people, especially people who were having a difficult time. He only made movies where terrible things happened. Mostly they were movies about problems—about victims of train accidents, or suicides, or missing persons—basically they were movies about people who didn't exist anymore. He made movies

36

about people's lives. He would go off with his camera and watch them as they grew sadder or older. Gawking, that's what it was. My father was a gawker. The fact that all his watching and gawking didn't make people any happier, well, he couldn't do anything about that.

11

When I saw Julia and Max again, three days later, everything was just the way it always was. None of the mothers at the playground would have thought Max had recently had his head bashed into a picture frame. This time, the two of them were really cheerful. Even Max smiled a little from under the hair hanging in front of his face and talked, talked, talked. He'd never spoken when I'd seen him at the playground before, but it didn't make that much difference, now that he did.

Because I couldn't understand a word he said.

It wasn't that much of a problem, because he wasn't actually talking to me. It was just that there was no saying who he *was* talking to. He was standing right under the fort and, unfortunately, it looked like he was talking to the air. The air doesn't answer when you speak to it though. Julia was doing the answering, except she wasn't exactly answering him, but me. She had climbed up to sit with me on top of the fort, and started by answering a question I hadn't even asked yet.

"You know who he's talking to, Mascha? Pablo."

"I don't see anyone."

"He's his imaginary friend. He talks to him all the time."

"That's odd."

"Daddy says so, too. He's actually told Max he can't talk to Pablo, but Max doesn't care. He talks to him anyway. Sometimes they fight."

"How would that work, exactly?"

"Max does it, believe me. So, do you want to play?"

"Play? Play what?"

"Let's pretend we're prisoners in the fort. We'll have a contest, and whoever wins won't be thrown to the bears. They're down in the moat. The other one will be devoured."

"Oh, okay. So what sort of contest?"

"We take turns saying things that are beautiful. First me, then you, then me again, then you. Whoever can't think of anything first, loses. You know, gets thrown to the lions."

"Or the bears."

"Exactly."

Max didn't seem to want anything to do with lions and bears. He quit talking to Pablo, and trudged off, lost in his own world. Eventually, he sat down on the carousel. I didn't really want to play Julia's game either. Thinking up beautiful things didn't really fit with what I'd seen lately. But by the time Max had sat down on the carousel, Julia had begun with her beautiful things, and I didn't have a choice. I had to play.

"The colors of duck wings, you know, the shimmery patches?"

"Hmm," I said, "the fog on the way to school in the morning."

"Being hugged, tightly," said Julia.

"Listening to music with my dad," I said.

"When Daddy's not around."

"When the batter of blueberry muffins slowly turns purple," I said.

"When it's morning and Max hasn't wet the bed."

"Um, okay," I said. "When someone smells good after a bath."

"A piece of melon."

"The streetlights near our house."

"Chickens," said Julia.

"Chickens?" I asked. "Hmm. The moon. Does that count? I already said streetlights."

"A picture with— Wait a minute, Mascha!"

And suddenly, just like that, the game was over. Julia jumped down from the fort and ran like a startled animal over to the carousel. I ran after her. Max had gotten himself into a fight, except that there was no one there for him to fight with, so he hit and shoved and throttled the air, and for the first time he was using words that I could understand: "Come here this instant!" he shouted. "Come right here and look at what you've done!" Max was red in the face. His hair was soaked with sweat and hung from his head in thick strands.

A couple of adults had gathered near the carousel, but not many, and most of the kids just sat in the sand still playing.

It was Pablo Max was shouting at, but since Pablo was invisible, the fight was eerie. Max growled, "Go on, go! Get out of here, why don't you? You'll be living in a home soon enough!" The mothers began to turn away and look after their children.

Julia stood blankly beside me, and I recognized the look on her face. It was the same one from a few days ago, at their house. She was absolutely still, but if you paid close attention, you could see she was shivering. You could hear her teeth going clackclackclackclackclack, muffled through her lips, which she pressed tightly together. Max continued to fight Pablo. I didn't want to imagine what Pablo would have looked like, if he'd had an actual body, or what he would have felt like, if he'd had an actual heart. The things Max shouted got worse and worse. "You fat slob! You miserable fatso! We never wanted you!"

Julia stopped shivering. She went over to Max and took several blows that were meant for Pablo. With her thin arms, which were covered up by long sleeves even though it was summer, she tried to calm her raging brother. She did it very quietly and seriously, almost like a grown-up.

"Let me go, let me go," Max screamed. "Leave me alone, you stupid cow!"

But Julia didn't let him go. She held him tightly with all her strength and said, just loudly enough for me to hear it, too, "It's okay, it's going to be okay, Max." And although it really wasn't okay, wasn't the least bit okay, Max slowly grew calmer in his sister's arms, until the last few head-shaking bystanders went away, one by one. In the end, I was the only person left to notice the way Julia stroked her brother's red face and quietly said, "You don't want that, do you? You don't want Daddy to hit you."

12

What happened at the playground reminded me that, of all the things I didn't like, the worst of them was being thirteen. There was nothing, absolutely nothing, you could do about the enormous zits on the sides of your nose. And you were expected to have a crush on someone, even if all the boys in your class looked and acted like ten-year-olds and all the older boys were totally out of reach. And no matter what you did, there was always some reason the grown-ups wouldn't listen to you. You were still considered a little kid, so nothing you said could possibly be important. Not when you were thirteen.

The stupid thing was, the things I'd been saying actually were important. It would have been nice to have had someone who would listen to me, despite the fact that I was only thirteen. I hadn't had much luck with my grandparents or my father, and I didn't really know anyone else. But one day after Max's fight, I decided to give it another try. I decided to head in the direction of the Brandners' and see who I met along the way.

I ran into a lot of people, at least for Clinton. Three. Only I couldn't really count the first one, this old guy on a bicycle who always tipped his greasy hat to me but never said a word. This time, too, he went by with nothing but a friendly whirr. The one who did speak to me was old Mr. Benrath, but somehow he didn't count either, because he was getting senile and definitely wouldn't be able to tell me anything about the Brandners.

"Mascha, would you like to come in? I'll make us a lovely cup of tea, with real cream!"

"Not today, Mr. Benrath. I've got to go. But thanks."

"Mascha, my child, just a small cup of tea, it won't take but a minute, really."

"No, really, Mr. Benrath. I can't. I've got to go."

"Nonsense. A small cup of tea. Are you coming in, then?"

"Next time, okay?"

Mr. Benrath was as old as everyone else in the entire neighborhood put together, and he stood all day long at his kitchen window, wrinkled, hacking and coughing. Whenever someone came by, he rushed out to his garden gate and asked with his last few ounces of breath if there was any chance they were headed to the newsstand, and if so, could they bring him back a pack of cigarettes.

Mr. Benrath must have lost a lot of money this way,

because he would give money to pretty much anyone. Some kids who lived nearby really did buy cigarettes with the money, but they'd never have dreamed of giving them to Mr. Benrath.

Since I was too young to buy cigarettes for him, he was always inviting me in to chat and have tea with real cream. Till then, I'd always said no. I was afraid I would suffocate there in his smoke-filled living room and never be heard from again. I didn't feel like suffering a smoky death, that day either, but even so, I turned and spoke to him.

"Mr. Benrath, do you know the Brandners? They live right across the way."

"Christian and Helen, isn't it? Right over there?"

"Do you ever hear them?"

"No, what do you mean?"

"But Mr. Benrath, you're almost neighbors. You must be able to hear something!"

"Mascha, won't you come in? I have tea."

Just for a moment, Mr. Benrath didn't look as confused as usual. His face seemed young and frightened, and he said to me, "Watch out, Mascha. They chased Elsa away because of that." And then, after those few Elsa-seconds, he turned back into the old Mr. Benrath again, wrinkled and coughing and offering tea with cream. But I didn't really hear him, because I had already said good-bye and gone on, even more confused than before.

13

If you're running away from a conversation with Mr. Benrath and you keep going, you have no choice but to pass by Mrs. Johnson's gate. Mrs. Johnson doesn't smoke and uses regular half-and-half from the supermarket—at least that's what I figured, because I'd never heard her say anything about cigarettes or cream. She has a different habit, which fits in very well with the neighborhood.

She tends her front garden.

But she doesn't just plant it once a year, like everyone else here. She does it once a week. When the flowers she's planted threaten to turn a week old, she rips them out of the ground and has her husband break up the soil so she can put in the next ones.

Because you can't spend the entire day ripping out flowers, Mrs. Johnson spends the rest of her time trying to give away the flowers she's ripped up to the same people who have just refused to buy cigarettes for Mr. Benrath. She was certainly the cheapest flower shop in the neighborhood, and, as usual, she didn't spare me her sales pitch.

"Come, child. Take a few asters."

"Grandma says we still have the ones from last week."

"Nonsense. They're yesterday's news."

"They look good, actually. Totally still red."

"Here, you can just take ten."

"They're still fresh, really."

"I'm putting a string around them for you."

"The ones at home still look fresh. Mrs. Johnson, you know everyone around here."

"It's deceiving. They only look fresh, but in reality, they're done for. Inside, they're withering."

"Mrs. Johnson, I want to ask you something."

"Oh, you poor thing. It's terrible what happened to your mother."

Mrs. Johnson was the person in the neighborhood who had kept up with the you-poor-things and the how-terribles the longest. Everyone else had stopped because I never answered them. I would have liked to have answered her that time, though. I even wished she would stroke my hair, and if she had, I would have said, *Stroke my father's hair, too. He hasn't had anyone do that for him in a long time.* But I didn't say anything because if I had, she would have given me three extra bouquets every time I passed.

Everyone in the neighborhood knew about my dead

mother because my mother had died in, of all places, Clinton, right in my grandparents' garden. She'd died in the garden with its picket fence, freshly painted, not a single slat broken. I think that was also the reason my father never wanted to come back here.

I hated that everyone knew about how she died. The people here hadn't known my mother any better than they knew me. But as I stood there with Mrs. Johnson and listened to her go on about her flowers, I suddenly didn't mind anymore. I decided to press her because I figured that a nosey person like Mrs. Johnson, who already knew everything about everyone, would know about the Brandners, too.

"The Brandner kids across the way, I think something's up with them."

"What, dear? What are you talking about?"

"I don't know, but I think the parents are doing something to them."

"Not the Brandners! What are you talking about? They were the king and queen of the spring festival just four years ago. We decorated the whole street just for them."

"I'm telling you, I actually saw it. Through the window."

"This keeps getting better. So you go around looking in people's windows, do you?"

"I heard screams, that's why. Mrs. Johnson, you must have noticed something. The Brandners live just across the street from you. Haven't you ever heard anything?"

"I'm going to tell you something. There was someone else here once, who suspected such a thing. She lived right next to the Brandners. Then two years ago, she moved away to her daughter's because she was so ashamed."

"Elsa."

"Elsa Levine, yes. How did you know? Well, it doesn't matter. At any rate, Elsa finally realized what people thought about what she'd said. It was slander. So watch what you say."

Mrs. Johnson looked furious. Her throat was red, and the tufts of grass she'd been holding lay on the ground. But she was also concerned. Maybe I seemed pale. Then she went on, more softly and quietly.

"My dear, it could be that there is screaming from time to time. The Brandners have problems with their children. It happens in the best of families."

"Yeah, problems, but not like this. This doesn't happen in the best of families."

"Well then, everyone must judge for himself. Besides, take a look. The children are fine. Julia and Max don't want for anything. Their clothes are always clean and there's a large garden behind their house. The Brandners are awfully nice people. Don't worry, everything is fine. The— Oh! Christian, hello. How are your lilies?"

He stood there, Mr. Brandner, maybe twenty yards away, on the small path beside his hydrangea patch. It was impressive how fast Mrs. Johnson was able to put a neighborly smile on her face. "So, are they wilting yet, Christian?"

It was also amazing the way Mr. Brandner replied, with a smile, "All good, Rose, all good. None of them hanging their heads yet at our house."

He seemed completely different from the way he'd been the last time I saw him. His face wasn't red. He was almost nice, even. I'm sure he was considered good-looking and friendly. He simply looked like a neighbor, chatting good-naturedly about lilies.

I felt like the net in a tennis game of words between Mr. Brandner and Mrs. Johnson, Mrs. Johnson and Mr. Brandner, back and forth and back again. I looked over at the Brandners' house and wondered if I had imagined it all. I wanted the answer to be yes.

Then I saw a curtain move in the window beneath the gable. It was only just barely noticeable, but I *felt* something. What I mean is, I felt it for real, all through my body, everywhere. I had no idea when, but at some point Mrs. Johnson had pressed a bouquet of asters into my hand. I raised my hand and pushed the asters back at Mrs. Johnson, hoping to spoil her pleasant conversation with Mr. Brandner. I knew no one here was really interested in Julia and Max.

14

ine.

One.

One.

Nineoneone.

I knew perfectly well you weren't allowed to call the police for just any reason.

Never call the police for fun, my grandmother had told me when I was a little kid. *They'll find out. They can tell who's calling. They'll find out in the end. They get upset when people play pranks on them, very upset, and they'll be upset with you.* But after my conversation with Mrs. Johnson, I didn't care if anyone got upset with me. All I wanted was for someone to pay attention to me.

The question was what I should actually say when I finally had a police officer on the line. *Hi, I'm Mascha, and could you please come rescue Julia and Max?* I sat myself down on the bed in the guest room for a long time, after talking to Mrs. Johnson, and thought about it.

Then I dialed the number, nine one one, but hung up without even waiting for the first ring. It wouldn't work. Nothing would work. I let my cell phone fall from my sweaty palm to the bed and lay there staring at it for ten minutes. I don't know what made me pick it up again, maybe the same thing that made me give Mrs. Johnson back the flowers, but finally I took the cell phone in my hand and dialed again: nine one one.

"Nine one one, what is your emergency?"

"Um, hello?"

"Who's calling?"

"I saw something."

"What is your name?"

"Mascha, Mascha Wernke. I saw something."

"Okay, just remain calm and tell me what you saw."

"I saw children, children with blue bruises and a cut on the head. I also saw . . ."

"Have you been involved in a fight?"

"Um, what?"

"What is it with you kids? We get these calls constantly. Three already today."

There's something about adult voices that totally throws me. There's this certain impatient tone they have. Sometimes I hear it from teachers or even the lady at the bakery. It cuts my words into tiny little pieces, and I begin to stutter, and I have nothing to say anymore because anything I'd say would sound ridiculous. It hadn't happened to me with the people I'd spoken to about Julia and Max so far, but the operator's voice was one of those word-chopping voices, and with every stuttered sentence that I sent out through the telephone line, I just made things worse.

"Um, yeah, no. I'm not just calling, see? I'm not just calling like that!"

"What is it then? Someone's gotten into a fight, is that it?"

"No, no one's actually getting beaten up right now. But it happened, you see. And, um, really, uh, often. It really happens very often. I think."

"Little girl, how old are you? Are you trying to play a joke?"

And then I did the dumbest thing I could have done. I began to laugh. That sometimes happened to me. At school one time, there was a teacher, the teacher who was in charge of recess. She came storming into our noisy classroom and yelled at us so badly that I burst into laughter out of fright. I was called up to stand in front of the classroom and got yelled at some more, even though I was the only one who had been sitting completely quietly just before, when all the other kids were making so much noise.

It was like that this time, too. I was so torn by what I was doing, so upset, that I couldn't help laughing. After that, I hung up. I had blown it, blown the whole thing.

I wasn't able to do it. I wasn't able to open my mouth at the right moment and make myself heard by the right people. Or by anyone at all. I'd made a few attempts, and I'd spoken to my grandparents, but there was no point. No one wanted to know anything about the people who owned the car dealership and how they beat their children so badly they had to spend their entire days hiding their wounds beneath long hair and long sleeves.

Time passed.

Weeks.

I was tired, just tired. Really, all I wanted was to be left alone, to be tired all by myself. To do nothing. That was all I wanted when I saw Julia and Max in the playground again one day. Julia turned to me with a deathly pale face.

"Do you want to run away?" she asked. "I really want to run away to someplace where no one will find us."

15

Julia's face was so pale that I was scared to respond. After a minute, on that sticky, hot afternoon, it wasn't clear to me anymore exactly what question she had asked. I just stared at her and said nothing.

"Mascha?"

"What? Oh yeah, do I want to run away? I don't know, probably not. How are you going to find a place like that, anyhow?"

"Maybe Canada. Or Madison. A kid who used to be in my class lives there now, and everything's always good with him."

"How do you even know?"

"You can just tell that kind of thing!"

"All right, then, Madison. It's a lot closer than Canada."

"We could take the bus. The bus goes everywhere. One time, we went—"

"What? Julia, did you run away before? Have you already tried it?"

"Are you nuts? We've never gone anywhere alone!"

The way Julia said that, both fearful and hopeful, and the noise that Max let out, which sounded like he had something to say on this subject—all of that made me suspect that Julia and Max had, in fact, run away before. But if they had, they hadn't gone far enough. Because they wouldn't still be here, in the playground showing their sad faces to the sun. Julia was sitting next to me on the fort, as usual, and Max was kneeling a few yards off in the sand and poking around with a red toy shovel that someone must have left behind. I couldn't see his face because he was sitting with his back to us. On his neck there was a great roll of fat, which somehow made me sad. I'd only seen rolls of flab like that on old men.

I sat there feeling numb. My arms, my legs, my thoughts, everything was numb. I didn't want to see Max go crazy or Julia get serious again. Mostly, I just wanted to be able to sit on my fort all by myself and listen to my music. That had always been enough before.

Not much more was happening on that early afternoon at the end of July. It was so hot. Every now and then something that you could hardly call a breeze passed us by. A couple of bees buzzed, a girl cried, and in the distance a car drove past. There were fewer mothers and children at the playground than usual. There was no shade there, but Max continued to kneel in the glowing-hot sand. It must have been painful, I thought, but he didn't seem to feel it, I guess because he was an expert at pain. Not even the hot sand could get a reaction out of him.

And then suddenly, on some sort of whim that surprised even me, I said to Julia, "Come on, let's play a game. Let's play Running Away."

16

lay Running Away? What do you mean?"

"You know, Running Away. Haven't you even done that before?"

"But how do you *play* it, Mascha? Either you run away, or you don't. You can't play it."

"We just have to imagine everything. First of all, something awful that we have to run away from. And then we imagine a knapsack that we've packed, and a map and then some money in case we get hungry on the way. We just have to imagine it all. And after we run away, we just come back."

"I don't know. Where should we go? I'm so hot."

"Don't worry. I know where. I know exactly where we can go."

I could tell Julia was thinking, *Just leave me alone, Mascha.* Her brother was kneeling peacefully in the sand, completely unaware.

"Maybe he wants to come along."

"Maybe he doesn't want to go anywhere."

"Maybe he wants to lie down on the sand and die because he hasn't done anything in such a long time." But then I added in a whisper, "I have a surprise for you. The place we're going to run away to, it's a surprise, and a secret, too." And with that, Julia became interested.

"A secret. Okay, a secret sounds good. Let's go."

So we went.

We played Running Away. We stomped through the sand and then slowly made our way along a path that only I knew about. I went first, Julia shuffled along behind me and last came Max, wheezing loudly.

The playground was at the edge of the neighborhood, so we didn't pass by many houses as we played our game. Because of the heat, the windows of the few houses we did pass were hidden behind blinds. There was no one out to see what miserable runaways we were as we trotted through the neighborhood.

Then we left the houses behind and came to a cornfield. The green stalks towered over us, and Max's wheezing grew louder. Then the corn became a field of grain, and everything around us shimmered gold.

The barley field. It was enormous, the size of three football fields. The stalks went up to our thighs, every one was the exact same height, and they went on forever. And right in the middle, in the middle of this giant field of grain, was a small blue wooden house. It wasn't much more than a shack, but there in the vast field of gold-gray-brown, it stood up like a too-tall cornflower. I said to Julia and Max, "There it is, see?"

Silence.

Julia was not the least bit impressed. When she found a few words for me, she simply murmured, "Oh, that. Everyone here knows that house. Everyone walking down the street can see it, but no one ever goes inside."

Even Max gave a disappointed nod. Who knew what he had imagined the secret spot would be—someplace with chocolate or something like that, not the edge of a field with a view of a useless blue shack that he'd seen a hundred times before. He pulled up a few stalks of barley, stripped off the kernels with his fingernails and threw them to the ground. Julia stood indecisively in the middle of the dusty path through the field.

"So, what now, Mascha?"

"Well, this is it."

"What are we supposed to do here? Stand around and look at that shack?"

"I haven't told you that part yet."

"Come on, Mascha, let's get out of here. We've been here before. Everyone knows about that house."

I had imagined it differently.

True, my idea of pretending to run away was not the best, but that blue house, it was really something. I wanted to cry or scream or throw myself down in the barley field. A few angry thoughts flew through my head, and I was about to say that Julia and Max didn't deserve a secret place like this, so come on, let's go. Then I saw Max's red face, which seemed to badly need a secret spot.

"Sure," I said. "Everyone knows about it. But only one person has the key, and that person is me."

17

had discovered the blue house two years ago, though it wasn't exactly a discovery, because I had always known about the blue house too. It was part of the neighborhood, just like the raked front yards and the barley field it stood in, and the green sea of corn growing between them.

So it wasn't that I had first *discovered* the house two years ago. More like that was when I'd come up with the idea that there were other uses for blue houses in barley fields than just looking at them. A person could, for example, fight through the stalks of grain, find that the door of the house was locked and then have the luck to find a rusty key under the large stone by the door. I was certain the blue house couldn't belong to anyone because it was so filthy inside and, after a little thinking, I came to the conclusion that effective immediately the house would have a new owner: me.

It was good that I had the key, because it seemed to make Julia and Max suddenly believe that this was a good place for us. It was a place where you could spend an entire afternoon. We followed the path to the edge of the field, turned left and walked a little farther before we actually entered the barley. I'd realized two years ago that if you wanted to keep a blue house in the center of a field a secret, you had to approach it as stealthily as possible. Every step in a field of grain leaves a footprint behind it, but those footprints could at least be made where they wouldn't be noticed.

Under our feet, the stems cracked. Over our heads, the sun burned. When we arrived at the house and I had unlocked the door, I heard someone say something bizarrely normal. It didn't seem possible that it was Max who cried out loud, "Oh man!" He shoved his way past me and then went carefully, slowly through the room, as if he were afraid he might break something by stepping on it. There wasn't much, just a few pieces of beaten-up furniture. When I first started using the house, I spent an entire week cleaning it. Back then, there had been nothing but a damp mattress, a scrub brush, an old rag and not nearly enough water, since it had to be hauled there by me in plastic bottles.

The whole room had been full of spiderwebs, which I'd removed from the corners with the help of some long sticks. I had taken the old mattress outside, beaten the dust out of it and dressed it up in an auburn-colored bed-sheet. I'd also cleaned the single window, which had been so filthy you couldn't tell it was a window anymore. Out-side the window there were iron bars, who knew why. Maybe someone had once stored something valuable here, maybe jewels or something, and they brought the mattress to use while keeping watch over it.

In the meantime, many more things had come to the blue house. Most of them things I had found on the street: the striped carpet with the fringe, the standing lamp that didn't have any place to plug it in, the small shelf and bleached-out painting in the gilt frame. In one corner was a bucket from the big cleanup, and on the shelf lay an old wool blanket, a stack of comics, a tin can full of cookies and a bottle of soda. I'd brought the cookies and the soda, which must have been boiling hot, at the very beginning of vacation, but they were still there because I hadn't been back to the blue house all summer.

I was used to this room, but when I saw Julia's and Max's reactions, I thought to myself that everything was really beautiful. It all fit so well together. Max said again, "Oh man!" The reddish-brown of the bedcover and the gilt-framed picture shone. I'd never really noticed it be-fore, but the shelf and lamp were in exactly the right spots. The room seemed like a place where a person could be safe—where Julia and Max could stay, just like that.

Julia actually seemed to feel at home there. She let herself plop down on the mattress.

"Mascha," she said. "This is crazy. Are the cookies still good?"

Max said nothing. He just stood there and smiled.

18

I t was hot in the room, and old and musty smelling. Many years of rainstorms had left the wood damp. I opened both the door and the window, but there was no breeze outside, so it didn't help much. Even so, the heat was different inside than out. It was easier to handle, and the smell was only bad for the first few minutes. Max was sweating, as usual, and his entire head was bright red, but his breathing was calm. He went to the bookshelf and took the comics down, one by one, like they were valuable.

Julia was still lying on the mattress and chatting away. Her mood had definitely improved. Max, who now had the tin of cookies balanced on the stack of comics, lay down beside Julia and began to read and chew. Since there was room on Julia's other side, I lay down beside them and said, "Odd to find such a house in a barley field, isn't it?"

"It's not that odd. Mama told me all about it."

"Your mama?"

"Sure, my mama. She said that there are places in the fields where nothing grows, where there's only sand. I think it has something to do with the ice age."

"The ice age, huh? But still, that's no reason for anyone to put up a house here."

"I don't know, Mascha. You've got to keep the tools somewhere."

"You mean like a thresher?"

"Maybe a very small one."

"This mattress was here when I found the house. Who needs a house with a mattress in it in the middle of a field? Did you see the grate over the window?"

"Maybe someone was locked up here. A princess?"

"Yeah, or a dragon."

"Or a grain thief. He was locked up right here in the field. Not bad."

Then Julia got quiet all of a sudden. After a while, she said if she had a house like this, she'd be here all the time. It had been different for me. It had been fun to clean the house up and furnish it. In the beginning, it had been fun just to be here—to read, listen to music, do nothing. The first few times, it was great. But then I realized I was even more alone here than I was at home with my deadly silent father, even more alone than I was in my grandparents' neighborhood, as empty as it was. More time alone wasn't what I needed, no thanks. And since I'd noticed that, I stopped coming so often. The best thing about the house was that it was there and that it was mine, whether I went there or not.

Max laughed out loud. His laughter sounded bright and happy, not like the laughter of someone who now and then fought with invisible friends. He took one cookie after the next from the tin, which now lay on his belly, and read the comics with shining eyes. Julia was also eating the cookies, and she suddenly wanted to know if I had my music with me. I gave her my music player, and she put in the earbuds and turned Leonard Cohen up so loud I could hear him, too.

I closed my eyes and whispered, "Baby, I've been waiting, I've been waiting night and day." It was my father's favorite song, "Waiting for the Miracle." I lay there and held my breath. With my eyes closed, I could see my father sitting excitedly in our kitchen and explaining the lyrics to me. I could hear him saying how there was this man who was in love with a woman and had been waiting for the longest time. He really didn't love her but he still wanted to marry her.

I lay there on the mattress, which was as old and musty as the house, listening to Max's laughter and Leonard's miracle. The whole time my father was sitting at our kitchen table, waiting for a miracle himself, but it wasn't ever going to come. He must have known that. Back when we first listened to that song together, my father had had tears in his eyes, and for a couple days afterward he holed himself up in his office. He was a person who cried. You never knew when he was going to lose it again. Sometimes all it took was a song. The odd thing was, as I lay there beside Julia and Max, my weeping father no longer made me feel sad. In the end, I thought the thing about the miracle never happening was different from what he'd said. Miracles really did exist—

When I woke up, everything was quiet. I don't know when I fell asleep or if Julia and Max had still been awake, but now they were asleep, and they looked so peaceful, the complete opposite of what they had been before.

I stood up, feeling groggy like I did when I slept too late in the morning. My eyes were burning. My head was still asleep. Only my legs were awake. But they might as well have been fast asleep, too. I didn't need them at the moment. I stood there, barely daring to breathe, in case it woke up Julia and Max. Max looked like a little kid. He breathed calmly and evenly, snoring quietly every now and then and twitching in his sleep. He was lying on his back and had a comic on his belly, along with about a thousand crumbs and the empty cookie tin. Julia still had the earbuds in her ears, but the music had stopped playing a long time ago. She was curled up, but not like someone who was afraid. More like someone who no longer had anything to fear, because there was someone standing guard outside.

And that was when I got the idea that I could protect them. I turned and crept to the door. Outside, the sun was lower and cast flickering shadows across the field. There was a light wind blowing, sending small yellow and gray waves through the barley. There was the sound of blackbirds and a car horn in the distance. There was my beating heart.

I closed the door.

Turned the key twice in the lock.

And then I ran.

19

On the way back to my grandparents' house, my cheeks were on fire, and it wasn't from the heat that still hung over the neighborhood. There were so many things I needed to think about, and it was amazing the way they all passed through my head in the short time it took me to run back. But most of all, I kept thinking I had saved Julia and Max, or at least I was about to. They wouldn't have to be afraid of anyone. I had taken care of that.

I ran and thought and ran and glowed. I was so happy that at one point, I almost fell down, but I wouldn't have cared if I had. Everything was going to be different now, all because I had locked the door of the blue house. There was a solution now, and I hadn't even needed to plan it. It just happened. No one would ever throw Max against a wall again, or hurt Julia's stomach, no one. I could have gone on thinking all this for hours, if I hadn't suddenly reached the house and come up against my grandmother's irritated gaze.

"Mascha, you're late! We were going to have a cookout tonight!"

My grandparents were sitting outside in the garden and had already begun to eat. I joined them and realized I was starving. But what about Julia and Max? They must be hungry, too, especially Max, who seemed to be made up entirely of hunger and rage. I thought about the cookies they had both eaten, and that calmed me down a bit. Cookies were better than nothing.

On the plate in the middle of our garden table there were hamburgers, and there was plenty of potato salad, too. Grandma always acted as if she were eating something at dinnertime, but really she only just picked at her food. And though my stomach was empty and growled loudly a couple of times, suddenly I could only pretend I was eating too. All I could think about was Julia and Max and how much better everything was going to be.

I didn't eat a bite. Normally, my grandmother would have said, *Why don't you eat, child? It's no wonder you're so small!* But that night she was busy asking me why I had been so late getting home instead, and whether I had seen those children.

"Uh, what children do you mean, Grandma?"

"The Brandner children you play with so much."

"Oh, them. They were only at the playground for a little while today. Then they left."

"Just the other day it seemed like they were so important to you."

"Yeah, we don't hang out as much anymore."

"Well, I have my knitting club tonight, and afterward we're going out for a glass of wine. And Grandpa is meeting up with his regulars at the bar. Will you be all right alone?"

"Sure. I'm really tired. I think I'll go to bed early."

"Good, then we'll see you at breakfast. And now, will you eat something?"

I had never been a good liar before. Before that afternoon at the blue house. Usually, whenever I tried to tell a lie, I got stuck somewhere in the story, because when you're lying, you have to make so many details line up. Really, all of them. Usually, I got embarrassed and stumbled over my lies.

Today was totally different. I was shocked at how easily and smoothly my lies flowed out of me, almost like the truth. When my grandmother had brought her plate into the kitchen and came back out into the garden, I was half-expecting her to say, *All right, Mascha, we're onto you. What have you done with the Brandner children?* But she didn't, she just reminded me to put the leftover hamburgers in the freezer and the potato salad in the fridge.

Which of course I didn't do. I waited till my grandmother had left and my grandfather had pulled the door closed behind him, and then I packed up the hamburgers, which weren't warm anymore, into a plastic container, and the potato salad into another one. From the cabinet, I took three bottles of water and two of my grandfather's chocolate bars, one semisweet and the other with nuts and raisins. I stuffed it all in my backpack along with two spoons, a wool blanket and two stuffed animals that my grandparents had kept in the guest room for years.

I'd seen in a movie once how someone who wanted to sneak out of his house at night stuffed his sheets to make it look like he was lying there asleep, so that's what I did, using all the T-shirts and pants that I could find in my suitcase. It probably wasn't even necessary, since my grandparents never looked in on me, but they might have made an exception that night, so I did it, just to be safe. I left the window of the guest room open, so I would be able to get back inside later. Luckily, my grandparents lived in a bungalow-style house, with everything on one floor.

Just as I was about to leave the house, it occurred to me that it would be dark in a couple of hours. In the blue house it would be pitch-black, which Julia and Max would definitely not like. I wouldn't have liked it either. I grabbed my grandfather's heavy old flashlight from the hall drawer and jammed it into my bag. Then, finally, I took off.

There was this pounding, pounding in my chest.

Everything else was quiet, just the sound of someone laughing in the distance. A dog barked. The night smelled of flowers and grilled meat.

20

There was a shortcut to the barley field, a more hidden way than the one I had taken with Julia and Max, but I decided to go the long way, through the neighborhood. Something drew me to the Brandners' house. I was curious to see what a house looked like where two adults had just discovered that their children were missing.

I saw more than the house. In front of the open door stood a thin woman who seemed afraid, almost like an animal. Under one of her eyes there was a large purple-yellow bruise, and when I looked at her, she quickly covered it with her long hair. From inside, I heard someone yelling: "They'll be sorry when they do come home! They'll find out a thing or two!" The woman saw that I'd heard it. She squeezed her eyes shut, sighed, turned around and went into the house. So that was her. Julia and Max's mother. *They'll be sorry when they do come home!* I could have told Mr. Brandner that he didn't have to worry about that anymore. They wouldn't be coming home.

I ran through the playground, passed the last few houses of the neighborhood and continued through the cornfield till I reached the enormous barley field. The sun hung low and orange. The whole sky was glowing, and here and there a crow flew across all the gorgeous colors. I was so happy for Julia and Max. They must have realized by now how good everything was going to be.

As I opened the door of the little house and went inside, I was nearly sick from an odor that hadn't been there before. It smelled like someone had crapped his pants, and I suddenly realized there was no bathroom. My gaze fell on the bucket in the corner, and I knew where the smell came from. Only then did I see their eyes, all four of them. Two of them were looking at me afraid. What I saw in the other two eyes was something entirely different—it was flat-out rage.

21

Where were you?" screamed Julia. "Where did you go, wherewereyouwherewereyou?"

I was glad I had locked the door behind me, or the two of them would have run away.

"Are you insane, are you an idiot, Mascha, why did you do that, why did you lock us in?"

Julia came at me right away, reached up to my shoulders and shook me, while Max said nothing, sat on the mattress and did nothing. He had his hands over his ears, but he must have been able to hear everything, because he flinched every time Julia spoke.

"Mascha, how could you lock us up like that? Are you crazy?"

"Um, so, just let me tell you what's going on. You have to listen to me!"

"What do you mean, listen to you? Just imagine what Daddy's going to do to us when we get home this late."

"He won't do anything. He knows you're here."

Perhaps the recommended course for those who don't lie well should simply be to start doing it, because starting with the second lie, everything becomes easy. You can calmly explain why the sky is blue, even if you have no clue. At least it was that way with me for my second lie. It just fell straight out of my mouth. Unfortunately, it was also completely idiotic. No one in the world would have fallen for it. I hadn't really thought about what I was going to say. I hadn't had the time. I'd just said something, anything, to make Julia stop. And she'd stopped, too. The second I said it, Julia fell silent. Then she asked, "What?"

I had two and a half seconds.

Two and a half seconds to think up a story that would make my lie believable, for why in the world would Julia and Max's father ever be okay with his kids living in a barley field? It would have to be a story that made everything make sense, it would have to be the best story there'd ever been, and for two and a half seconds the characters in it swirled around in my brain—my grandparents with their evening glasses of wine and my father back home at the kitchen table and the bellowing Mr. Brandner and above all Mrs. Brandner, standing in front of her house afraid with her eyes closed, Mrs. Brandner with the purple-yellow face, Mrs. Brandner—

And then I knew what I had to say. I took a breath and blurted out, "Your mother had to go to the hospital." It was easy to say it, and it must have been easy to believe it, too, because Max began to whimper and Julia's face got serious and stiff.

"How do you know that?" she asked. "Mama's fine!"

"I bumped into your father on the way home, and he told me."

"What did he say? Did you see her? Was she bleeding again? Did she look bad?"

"She was already in the car. I didn't see her. Your father wanted to leave right away and was glad that he'd seen me."

"Mama."

"Julia, there's definitely nothing serious wrong with your mother. She just needed to go to the hospital to get checked out or something. And your dad asked me to look after you."

"Here?"

"You can't come to my Grandma and Grandpa's because they're not there right now. You have to stay here for now."

"But it stinks here, Mascha. Max is scared, and me, too. And we're hungry. Do you have anything to eat?"

"Yep, your parents were grilling, and your dad asked me to bring you some."

"Mascha, I don't get it. Usually we're always alone with Daddy when he . . . when Mama . . . when something's up with Mama."

"I don't know why he asked me. There was no one else there. I wondered about it too."

So I didn't have to go on any longer, I began pulling the plastic containers out of my backpack, and Julia looked at them, confused.

"Mascha, where are those containers from? Ours are different."

I pretended like I didn't hear the question and brought out the water and chocolate. It was darker now, but we didn't need lights yet, so I left the flashlight in the bag, just took the spoons and handed them out.

Julia sat down beside her brother on the mattress and divided up the food so that each container had the same amount of potatoes and hamburgers. Max spooned up the potato salad hungrily but it seemed he was afraid of the hamburgers. First, he poked at one carefully with his index finger, then finally took a bite and ate it slowly.

Julia ate carefully, too, but with her it seemed less out of fear than that she was using manners that were way too formal for the little house and its smell. I realized that Max had snatched up one of the chocolate bars without my seeing it, and was now sitting on it. I hoped he had picked the nuts-and-raisins one, since the dark one wasn't really sweet enough to even count as chocolate. I probably shouldn't have even brought it.

As I watched Julia and Max eat, the small patch of blue behind them grew darker, the sky all cut to bits by the bars on the window. The soda can on the shelf was empty. I thought about the hot, sticky liquid and pushed one of the bottles of water toward the mattress. Julia grabbed it and drank it half down.

Then I smelled it again.

The stink that I knew from the subways at home.

I couldn't imagine anything more revolting than the bucket that stood in the corner, unless it was taking it in my hand, going outside and emptying it. But I had to do it. Otherwise, there was no way Julia and Max could stay there. The two of them were eating without paying any attention to me. I breathed through my mouth as I took up the bucket and unlocked the door. I dumped it out as quickly as I could into the field and hoped the barley wouldn't later be used to brew my grandfather's beer.

When I returned to the house, everything was just the same, only dimmer. Julia saw me and the bucket in my hand and said quietly, "Thank you."

Meanwhile, Max focused on his chocolate. The bitter flavor of the dark chocolate didn't seem to bother him. He'd liked the food, but even so, he seemed sad. His face was wet like he'd been crying, without my even noticing.

The mood in the blue house was so depressing that I decided to pull out the blankets, stuffed animals and flashlight. I undid the zipper of my backpack loudly.

"Here," I said to Julia, "for tonight, and so you have some light. I'll be back again first thing tomorrow morning."

Julia looked so worn out and when she opened her mouth to speak, she said nothing. I said good-bye and left quickly so they wouldn't be able to ask me any more questions, like why I hadn't brought them their own stuffed animals.

It wasn't really dark out, but the dim sky with its gray haze and the songs of the owls and the crickets made the evening feel suddenly spooky. Luckily, Julia and Max wouldn't see or hear much of that, not from inside their house. The air had grown cooler, and I felt a breeze across my face. I ran, first between the prickly rows of grain, then along the path through the field and finally through the neighborhood. I ran till I was in my grandparents' garden and then climbed through the window back into their guest room.

My heart pounded. Julia and Max, and Max and Julia, and the darkness, and the field, and the wind in the barley. Along with my heart, I felt the pounding of a bad conscience. I thought of how frightened they must be and how worried their mother must be. The one thing that helped my bad conscience was the image of the brightly lit Brandner house, which I'd run past again on the way home, and the small cluster of people gathered in front of it, whispering quietly among themselves. Mr. Brandner had stood out in front of the door with his wife, making himself out to be the kindest, most caring father in all of Clinton.

22

The night was long. It just wouldn't end. If I was able to sleep at all, it was for a couple of hours at most. The rest of the time I lay there, wide awake, tossing and turning. What I really wanted to do was get up and go back to the blue house, but I was also hoping that Julia and Max were asleep, and I didn't want to wake them. I lay there thinking that nothing in the world takes longer than night turning into day. It happened so slowly I wanted to scream, but I didn't, because I'd never heard of a night that forgot to end.

In the dark, I made a thousand plans, most of which seemed silly by dawn. In the morning, only one idea was left: to go to the bakery and get Julia and Max some breakfast.

It was still very early as I put on my sweats and sneakers and left a note saying: *Gone jogging.* I tried to imagine how perplexed my grandmother would be when she found the message. She would shake her head and then go into the kitchen with a shrug. I had never once gone jogging in all the time I'd been coming to Clinton. Truth be told, I'd never in my life jogged willingly at all. I only had the sweats because they were comfortable, and the sneakers were just what I wore every day.

I set the note on the table in the hall, put some money from my wallet into my sweatpants pocket and left the house. The early quiet was nicer than the quiet in the middle of the day. At seven o'clock in the morning, it was supposed to be quiet.

There was almost no one around, just two roofers standing in front of a house, propping a ladder up against the side of the building. I walked for ten minutes through the neighborhood, but this time didn't pass the Brandner house because the bakery was in the opposite direction. I could have stopped at the newsstand where Mr. Benrath got his cigarettes, but I knew the owner there, and he might wonder why I was craving breakfast things; and anyway, I didn't think he carried breakfast things.

I didn't know the bakery lady, but unfortunately Mrs. Johnson was there, peering through the glass at the pastries. She had her back to me and studied each item closely, then finally said, "Four rolls, Margie, the usual."

I entered the shop quietly, without saying good morning, so that Mrs. Johnson wouldn't notice me. Between us on line was an old man with a tiny cloth shopping bag in his hand, shifting his weight from one foot to the other.

It looked like he had to go to the bathroom and wouldn't take long to make his purchase, which was exactly the way it went—just an almond croissant and a quick exit. I should have been able to make my order in peace—two poppy-seed swirls and two cinnamon swirls and two chocolate milks—but then Mrs. Johnson, who had spent the past several minutes peering into her pocketbook, turned around and discovered both her wallet, still lying on the counter, and me.

"You're certainly up early, my dear. Are Grandma and Grandpa still sleeping?"

"Uh, good morning. Yeah, they're asleep. I wanted to surprise them with some pastries."

"That's a lovely idea! Well, go ahead, make your order. I have something I want to talk to Margie about."

"No, no, I have time."

"Just a moment, dear. By the way, you know the Brandners' children, don't you? Did you play with them yesterday?"

"Just for a little while, before lunch. Why?"

"Oh, I was just wondering. So you didn't see them again after that?"

"No, Mrs. Johnson."

"Did they say anything to you?"

"Like what sort of thing?"

"Hmm, well, never mind. How many rolls are you buying then?"

"Uh, I don't know."

And though no one had asked her, Mrs. Johnson turned to the bakery lady and said, "Margie, pack up six rolls for the little one here, that should do."

I started to object, but the bakery lady took a paper bag and loaded it with the rolls that I didn't want. I stood there with my bag and couldn't do a thing about it because Mrs. Johnson wouldn't leave. When she went back to rummaging around in her handbag, I said as quietly and as quickly as I could, "And two poppy-seed swirls and two cinnamon swirls and two chocolate milks," but when it was all added up, I was nineteen cents short.

I wanted to put back the rolls, but there were too many people in the neighborhood who knew my grandmother's diet and knew she would never in her life eat something sweet for breakfast. Mrs. Johnson thankfully came to my rescue and laid the missing coins on the counter.

The shop had gotten crowded while this was happening, and the people were all watching me. I wondered whether Julia and Max were awake yet, and if they were hungry. I grabbed my bags, said good-bye without even looking at Mrs. Johnson and fled the shop. I ran all the way to the playground, where I was waved at by the old man on the bicycle who always seemed so glad to see me.

I was actually jogging, so it would look like I'd gone out for a run and to get the bread, but I was worried because Mrs. Johnson would definitely mention the whole thing about the rolls to my grandmother. What then? I didn't care. The important thing now was to get Julia and Max something to eat as quickly as possible. Especially Max.

When I arrived at the blue house, soaked with sweat because I'd run so fast, Max really did look like some poor child who was dying of hunger. He was cowering at the back of the mattress, wrapped tightly in the woolen blankets, and he was crying, crying, crying, but I couldn't make out his words. Julia sat beside him and rested her forehead on his shoulder. His sobs jostled her head, but Julia stayed there with him. After a while, she said loudly, "No one is going to give you a bath. No one!"

Suddenly, I understood what he'd been wailing: *No bath! No bath.* A bath must have been a horrible thing for him. I couldn't understand it because I had always liked taking baths, but I guess Max saw baths differently. For him the idea of a bath was so awful that Julia couldn't calm him down at all.

I stood there a while before either of them noticed me. As soon as they did, Julia began to talk. She wasn't looking at me, but what she said was definitely intended for me to hear. She spoke the way some kids recite poetry for school: like a robot. Her poem went like this: "Max went in the bed, do you understand, Mascha, he went in the bed."

"Yes, okay, Julia, he went in the bed, I get it."

But I guess I didn't understand at all what it meant to them for Max to pee in the bed. Maybe it meant that Max would be shoved by his father into a bath full of very hot water. The fact that there was no tub in the blue house, not even a washbasin, didn't stop Max from screaming. There was so much fear in his face, red, wet-faced fear.

He finally got quiet, but just for a minute, and I asked, "What are we going to do?"

Julia, still pressing her forehead to Max's shoulder, repeated weakly, in a mechanical voice, "Yes, what are we going to do?"

23

I don't know how long I listened to Max's screaming. When I couldn't take it anymore, I said, "I'm going to get some dry clothes and things. Here, eat breakfast."

I left the house and took my shortcut, running through uncut fields and leaping over holes in the ground, to my grandparents' house. When I got there, I was sweating and out of breath, so my grandparents totally believed that I'd been jogging, and I didn't have to dream up another story, which was a good thing—my head was too full of them already.

I had to get dry clothes for Max and a new bedsheet. Julia and Max needed water for drinking and bathing. I also planned to take some sausage and cheese from the fridge for the rolls, which turned out not to be such a bad thing to have, after all. A day could be long, and they would be hungry. But just then, I couldn't think about any of those things, because I had to sit down and have breakfast with my grandparents and pretend like everything was normal.

I could tell my grandparents knew all about Julia and Max's disappearance. In this neighborhood, everyone knew everything about everyone, and that included missing kids, even if they were kids nobody ordinarily cared about. I'm sure Trudy had told her something. She always had some new gossip for my grandmother, and she would come by first thing in the morning to share it. Trudy must have been there, because my grandmother stirred her coffee and finally said, with a strange look in her eye, "Apparently, your friends have run away. What do you know about it?"

"What friends? Julia and Max? What do you mean they ran away?"

"They didn't come home last night."

"Oh."

"Their parents are extremely upset. Trudy says she's never seen Helen Brandner in such a state."

"But what do you mean they ran away? How do you know?"

"There's no way of knowing for certain, but two years ago they did the same thing. The little one was no older than five at the time. They got on the train and went all the way to South Carolina. That's a ten-hour trip, at least."

"South Carolina? That's weird. They've never mentioned South Carolina."

"Their aunt lives there. Their mother's sister. Near Greenville."

"Greenville?"

"Tell me, Mascha. They must have said something to you. They must have told you their plans."

"All I do with Julia is listen to music. And Max never says anything at all."

"Hmm. Well, at any rate, the children are missing. The whole neighborhood's talking about it."

"What are the Brandners doing?"

"They haven't been able to get ahold of the aunt, but by now the children must have gotten there. The police have been notified. Trudy says they're just waiting. It's almost certain they know where they've gone, but I think Helen also called a few children from the school."

I looked up at my grandfather. He was eating an apple in a way that only a grandfather can eat an apple. He held it in one hand and used the other to cut off small pieces with a fruit knife. He was eating them from the tip of the blade. It made me worry he was going to hurt himself. But he didn't; he did something entirely different: he spoke. With his mouth full, he said, "It's no wonder they've run away."

My grandmother hissed sharply, "John! We said we were going to keep out of it!"

And with that, the subject was closed. Grandma had a tight grip on Grandpa. Dad had told me as much, and I'd seen it for myself many times. The truth was, I was happy to hear what my grandmother said because it meant I didn't have to come up with any more Julia-and-Max lies, and on top of that, my grandfather had *said* something. He had admitted that he knew something.

About the blue bruises.

The screams.

I wasn't sure how news of the bruises and screams had spread through the neighborhood, or exactly what my grandfather knew, but he clearly knew something, and that was good. If it had been the day before, I probably would have pestered him to explain what he meant, but everything was different now, so I just spread jelly over my roll and went to search through my T-shirts and pants for something that Max could wear.

I looked through the clothes I'd used to stuff my bed-sheets the night before and found plenty that he could wear, but when I held them up, I realized that Max and his belly would never fit into my clothes. I felt my face turn red and my ears were ringing. I didn't know what to do. Max was sitting there in the blue house in wet clothes, on a wet sheet, and I didn't have a clue how I could help him. I took my purple leggings, because at least they were stretchy, and went into my grandparents' room to look for a bedsheet in the closet. I took a flat one. It smelled like it came from a tidy world where nothing bad ever happened to anyone.

Once I was in the closet, I noticed my grandfather's shelves.

There was one shelf with pants, one with sweaters, one with T-shirts. All of them would be much too big for Max, but they would fit him better than my things. At least they would go over his belly. I took a pair of worn, dark green corduroys from the bottom of the shelf, plus a pair of suspenders and a pale yellow T-shirt that said *Together in Clinton*, the town's slogan. I took some underwear, too, after debating whether it would be strange for Max to wear them, but in the end I decided it would be stranger if he didn't have any.

Meanwhile, I could see through the bedroom window that my grandparents were outside in the garden. Grandma was hanging the wash on the line, and my grandfather was weeding. They both looked odd to me, the way people sometimes do when you see them through glass. I opened the window and called, "I'm going out, I'll be back for lunch."

Then I ran through the house and packed a couple plastic bottles of water, a washcloth, a hand towel and soap into the bag with the clothes. I took cheese and cold cuts and a plastic bowl I found in the kitchen and got some paper and pencils and two books from the guest room and then I headed off. I was able to go right out the front door with my bag and the bowl without raising any suspicions because everyone who might wonder about the things I had with me was out in the back garden. But that wasn't entirely true. I couldn't pass by the Brandners' house—not with the bag, not with the bowl. So I decided on the shortcut, though I was curious to see what was happening at Julia and Max's just then.

24

When I opened the door to the blue house, I was hit by the familiar smell of a toilet and a feeling of sadness—dark, sticky sorrow, and it was worse than before. The mattress was propped up to dry against the wall. Max was still wrapped in the blanket but now he was naked underneath, and his clothes lay wadded up with the sheet in a pile by the shelf. He wasn't screaming anymore, just whimpering. Julia had laid her hand on his heaving shoulder and was whispering to him, just like she had at the playground: "It's going to be all right. It's going to be all right."

Over and over.

"It's going to be all right."

But it wasn't all right. It was horrible, the smell and the sadness.

"I have everything here," I said, with fake cheerfulness. "Some things to put on, some things for washing up, and even some men's shower gel for the well-groomed gentleman."

"I won't!" Max shouted. "I won't, I won't!"

But Julia was firm and said, "You're going to do it, Max, or I'll do it for you!"

Slowly, Max dropped the blanket from his shoulders. Though Julia shielded him like a bodyguard, I could see plenty of him, because there was so much of Max that protruded beyond her edges.

Oh God.

No.

Max's behind and back had been so badly beaten that there was hardly any normal skin left. On the insides of his arms, on the backs of his thighs, everywhere, there were scabs and welts and blue bruises, some darker, some lighter. On the back of each buttock there was a wide stretch of red, and I saw that his feet were red, too.

I'm not really the sort of person who gives other people hugs—no one ever taught me how to do that—but at that moment, when I saw Max's body, I wanted to hug him. I wanted to hug him so tightly that no one would ever dare hurt him again.

But instead I just stood there with a sick feeling in my stomach. And then I began to cry. Tears ran down my cheeks and into the corners of my mouth. So they didn't notice, I quickly turned and began to fill the bowl with water. "Here you go," I said, and pushed the bowl, washcloth, towel and shower gel toward them.

I squatted in a corner—not the one with the stinking bucket—and watched Max wash. Julia, who was still being very kind to him, urged him to hurry. Max washed his legs and backside quickly and quietly, with a shocked expression. For a few seconds, Max turned his face toward me, and I could see how unpleasant bathing was for him, but somehow I could also sense him relaxing. Before, I imagined, the water had always been too hot and his father had just beaten him.

When he was finished washing, Julia handed him the towel and told him to dry himself. I stood up from my corner and went to get the dry clothes from the bag. The things looked even more grandfatherly now than they had before on the shelves. They were just terrible. I brought them to Max and expected him to refuse to put on such hideous ill-fitting things, but it didn't seem to bother him. It was only Julia who looked at the clothes with hatred.

When Max was dressed, I began to cry again. I couldn't help it. He looked awful, like a clown. His wounded body was covered in a T-shirt that reached to his knees, and beneath that his fat legs were squeezed into my purple leggings.

Together in Clinton.

So I wouldn't have to look at him anymore, I grabbed

the bowl and the stinking bucket and muttered, "I'm going to take these outside. I'll be right back." Once I'd locked the door from the outside and taken a few steps into the field, I poured out the bucket and watched the yellow liquid soak into the stalks of barley. It was less disgusting than the day before, but I certainly could think of nicer things to do on the first afternoon of August.

I washed out the bucket with the bathwater. As I went back toward the house with the bowl and washcloth in one hand and the bucket in the other, I stumbled. It was just a small stumble, over my own feet, nothing. But all at once, I was overcome with rage.

A rage that was bigger than the barley field.

Bigger than the cornfield beside it.

Bigger than anything.

I slammed the bucket against the side of the blue house, and then the bowl, which amazingly didn't even crack. The bucket was almost okay, except for a tiny dent. Then I kicked the door, four, five, six times. I only stopped when the pain in my foot was too much.

"Dammit," I screamed, with tears running from my eyes, and since I couldn't think of a better word, I shouted it again.

"Dammit!"

And then I went back into the house. Julia was just spreading my grandparents' white bedsheet over the

99

mattress, which was back in its old place on the floor, though it couldn't have been dry. Then she turned to me with the same look of fury she'd had the day before. This time there was also fear.

"You'll be sorry," she whispered, and I could hear her voice tremble. "You'll be sorry if you tell anyone what you saw."

25

My face turned red. I didn't really feel like responding to that, but Julia, who was sitting on the mattress with Max again, looked at me furiously, waiting. I had to say something.

"Julia. The way he looks. Someone has to do something."

"No they don't. Everything is fine. When Daddy whips us, he has a reason. Mascha, promise me! Promise me you won't tell anyone."

"Why should I promise you that? I've seen Max. I've seen what happens at your house."

"There's nothing wrong. When we bother Daddy, he whips us. That's it. Max is the one who bothers him the most, because he's still little. Little kids bother people more. Just yesterday, Max—"

"Julia?"

"Yeah?"

"Tell me something—"

"What?"

"Do you cry?"

I could see Julia didn't like this question, but it was too late. I had asked it. Looking hurt, Julia pulled my music player out of her pants pocket, put the earbuds in her ears and turned Leonard Cohen up so loud that Max, who was sitting beside her, stopped chewing his fingernails to jam his fingers in his ears. She sat like that for an entire song, staring straight ahead like she was somewhere far away, and then she ripped out the earbuds, looked at me and said gruffly, "I never cry. I'm used to it."

"How can you get used to it? I can't even imagine."

"It's easy. Because, Mascha, most of the time, I'm not even there."

"What do you mean?"

"It's like this. I'm not there. When Daddy hits me, I find a spot on the wall, and I look at it the whole time. I imagine that I'm somewhere else, and it works. When Daddy has one of his fits, I'm always somewhere else. I don't notice anything, because I'm just not there."

"And when he beats Max? You do the same thing?"

"Yeah."

"Couldn't you help him?"

"This way, it's over faster. Whenever I say anything, it just makes Daddy madder. I used to try to stop him, but not anymore. Only Mama tries to do that sometimes. She tries to distract him, so he hits her and not us. That's the only time I do something. I try to distract him myself, so he doesn't hit Mama."

"But Julia, hasn't anyone ever seen this happening? Don't you ever go to the doctor?"

"Hardly ever, and when we do, it's always to a new doctor. One time one of them said something, and Daddy got really mad and threatened to take him to court."

"Julia?"

"Stop it."

"Julia. Why can't I tell anyone?"

Julia jumped up from the mattress and stood directly in front of me, hyperventilating. Max was sitting on the mattress and chewing one of the dry rolls, but he looked panicked, too. Then something amazing happened. While Julia sat there boiling, Max began to speak.

Not with Pablo.

Not with Julia.

He spoke to me.

"We would have to leave," he announced. "We would have to go to a home. Daddy would send us to a home if you told, and Mama would be dead. Mama will be completely dead if you tell."

26

ompletely dead. That was how he put it. Completely dead. It was as if Julia had given Max a voice to say what she couldn't. I listened to Max speak and understood everything. Or maybe I didn't understand at all. After a while, Julia remembered how to talk. She looked wounded.

"Mascha, you can't. You can't tell. Don't you get it? We don't want to go to a home. We don't want Mama to die."

"Your father told you that? Maybe that's not what he meant."

"Yes it is. Believe me, everything would be awful. One time, someone tried to help us—Mrs. Levine from next door. It was horrible. Daddy thought we had told. Mascha, everything will be horrible if you tell."

"It can't get much worse than it is."

"Yes it can. If Mama wasn't there, that would be worse."

Max had now discovered my bag and was rummaging

around in it. He put the paper and pencils on the mattress, threw the books down and took out the package with the cold cuts. He wrapped a slice of cheese around the remainder of a roll and said quietly, "Mama."

Julia's voice was louder. "Can't you just tell us what happened to Mama?"

I thought about the people I had seen in front of the Brandners' house last night, and the people who had probably come there today.

"There's no one at your house," I told her. "Your parents aren't back from the hospital. Your father will call me as soon as he gets back home."

"I don't get it. Why do we have to stay here? Why can't we go out?"

"That's the way your dad wanted it."

"But I don't get it. And why hasn't he called you to tell us what's going on with Mama? We're afraid that she . . . um . . . we're afraid that she's dead."

"She is not dead, Julia. Believe me, I know. Your mother is not dead. Only mine is."

"You have a dead mother? The whole time you've played with us at the playground, you've had a dead mother?"

"The whole time. I have a father who's still alive, but I don't hear from him much."

I was ashamed of myself for using my dead mother to win them over. Julia and Max had much bigger problems than I did. Much. It gave me a strange feeling, but I did it: I told them my story. It just seemed to shoot out of me. I talked and talked and talked. The words fell from my mouth. I told Julia and Max about the scrambled eggs I made for my father and me so that we had something hot to eat at least once a week. I told them how he was only happy when he talked on the phone with his documentary-film colleagues, and how he didn't have any happiness left over for me. Julia and Max listened to it all: how the people from the neighborhood had stood there at my grandparents' garden fence, watching, as my mother was carried away, and how weirdly they treated me after, like I was an alien or something. I told them how my father didn't make it out of bed some days, and how I had to shake him and pull on him when I knew that he had some important appointment. I explained how alone I felt. All this would normally have been pretty embarrassing for me, but Julia took my hand.

She said to Max, "Come here." And when he came, she laid her right hand on top of both of ours and whispered, "We promise, Mascha. We promise we will never tell anyone in the entire world what you've told us. Max and I promise you."

"It's all right, you can tell anyone you like. No one would care. Especially not Grandma and Grandpa."

"Mascha, we promise! And you have to make a promise

to us. Never tell anyone what you've seen. Or what we told you. Do you understand? Come on, Mascha, say it!"

"Yeah, but—"

"Please, Mascha!"

"All right. Okay. I promise."

I left the house with the wet things and passed by the Brandners' on my way to have lunch at my grandparents'. I realized that my promise had created a new problem for me. If I couldn't tell anyone else about Mr. Brandner's beatings, it meant that I was the only person in the world who could help Julia and Max. It made everything harder. Would the two of them have to stay in the blue house forever? Would something terrible happen to them if they left because no one in the neighborhood would even notice what was going on? If I didn't think of something, and soon, how could I let them leave the blue house?

27

Blue.
Red.
Blue.

The light on the police car that was parked in front of the Brandners' was spinning so fast it made me dizzy. I counted three cars with flashing lights, but I couldn't count the people crowded around the Brandner house. There were too many. My heart was pounding in my ears again. I had wrapped Max's wet clothes in the bedsheet and jammed the whole bundle into my bag, so I didn't look suspicious.

As casually as I could, I joined all the bystanders. Everyone was talking to one another. At first I couldn't make out what they were saying. Then I concentrated on the conversation that was going on directly to my right, between two old women I knew by sight. They both reeked of the same perfume Grandma used.

I tried to make it seem like there was something I

wanted to look at so they wouldn't notice I was eavesdropping on them, and it worked. I heard everything I
wanted to and more—I heard what I didn't want to hear.

Everyone still believed that Julia and Max had run
away, but since they couldn't be certain if they were
nearby or far away, they had called the police to help
search for the children. Apparently, Mr. Brandner didn't
want to involve them, but Mrs. Brandner insisted.

When I heard that, my heart beat so hard it almost
fell right out of me. They were searching for them. Oh
God. They would find Julia and Max in less than an hour.

The blue house was more or less just around the corner, right under the noses of all these people. A person
would have to be blind and deaf not to realize it was a good
place for runaway kids. Even for kids who just wanted to
play runaway, and didn't actually want to stay in the blue
house at all. One of the women was saying that the police
were going to look in the old mill at the edge of town first,
and then in the woods on the west side of town, and that
they had already begun to search the surrounding towns.
I breathed again. *Surrounding towns* sounded good to me.
Anything to do with *surrounding* sounded especially good
just then.

I looked at all the people and had no idea why they
were there. Their eyes shined. It was like they were happy
something had finally happened here.

Next to me, one man whispered, "No one wants my

opinion, but if you ask me, something like this was just waiting to happen." Someone else hissed, "Shhh!" Up front, another voice said quietly, "That poor woman. Can you imagine what she's going through?" Someone else said, "The staff from the car dealership are all out looking for them, too."

Suddenly, I'd had enough. I wanted to get out of there. Besides, I really had to get back home. My grandmother tolerated no nonsense when it came to her food getting cold. I'd been late for dinner the night before, and eventually a woman like my grandmother was going to run out of patience.

I was late, but I didn't hurry. My pulse raced anyhow. It was clear things couldn't go on the way they were. If I didn't do something, the police would soon discover Max and Julia and who knows what would happen then. I figured they might be all right where they were until morning, but I needed a new hiding place for them and quickly. In my mind, I searched the entire neighborhood for a few square yards that no one would find. I stared at the asphalt as I walked, and it was only when I arrived home that I saw the police car parked in front of my grandparents' house.

28

dgar, it's nothing!" I heard Grandma say as I stood in the hall, my knees weak. She was using the exaggerated happy voice that she usually only put on for the July birthday parties. "We don't always eat at exactly the same time. Really, Edgar, we're not like that. Perhaps a little glass of something?"

I went quickly to my room and stuffed the wet things into the laundry basket. When I went into the kitchen, there were three pairs of eyes directed at me, but surprisingly, none of them seemed angry. Even my grandmother kept her fake cheer and called out, "Mascha, dear! It's good you're home!"

"Grandma. I was just at the playground. I lost track of time."

"Oh, don't worry. This is Edgar. He's with the police. He would like to ask you a few questions about Julia and Max. I already told him you hadn't heard anything, that you didn't know a thing. That's what I told him."

"Yeah, that's right. I don't know anything. Except that they're gone. That's what everyone's saying."

"Edgar—I mean Officer Price—would like to know if you've noticed anything, even if you haven't seen much of them lately."

The police officer named Edgar cleared his throat. Grandpa sat beside him, drumming his fingers quietly on the kitchen table with absolutely no birthday airs about him.

"Now then, young lady," said the policeman very slowly, "think carefully. Did the children ever mention any particular place to you? Anyplace at all. Anything you can remember will be helpful."

"Grandma asked me that already. But really, I never heard them mention anyplace. They didn't talk much to start with."

"But perhaps they made some sort of offhand remark. We're almost certain they've run away. You might be able to help us find them more quickly."

"But I don't know anything. I said that already."

"Young lady, just imagine: the parents waiting up all night for some sign. They're sick with worry. You may understand it better later, when you have your own children."

"But what can I do about it?"

"Julia and Max have run away a few times before. Most of the time, they've come back home late at night, but once they showed up at their aunt's house the following morning."

"So then they'll be home soon. If that's what they always do."

"Perhaps. But it would be better if they came back right away. So think. Try to remember! Please try to think of anything that might be important."

While he talked, I stared at the kitchen cabinets, avoiding the threat in his gray eyes. But as soon as I realized what I was doing, I looked straight at him. I didn't want him wondering about my weird fascination with the cabinets. My grandfather continued to drum his fingers anxiously on the table and looked at me with a surprised sort of horror that I couldn't quite explain. It was almost as if with his strange look he wanted to ask me something like, *What about what you told us before?* But even if he had said it, I would have had to answer, *What? I have no idea what you're talking about.* I had promised Julia and Max not to tell anyone about the bruises I'd seen, *not anyone*, and I held myself to that. I was going to hold myself to that promise forever.

Before, it had been different—before this summer I hadn't taken promises very seriously. But now, now my word mattered.

It mattered that no one died.

It mattered that no one had to go to a home.

It mattered that no one got suspicious.

I had to get away from the question in my grandfather's eyes, so I looked back at the policeman named Edgar, but he wasn't looking at me anymore—or not at my face. He was looking down, directly at my feet, and when I happened to look there too I saw why. There, stuck to my right sneaker, were two perfectly formed heads of barley.

"You know what?" I said, bringing the policeman's gaze back up. "I remember something now. Julia mentioned Madison one time. It just popped back into my head."

29

After lunch, Grandpa stood up silently and disappeared, which I don't think had anything to do with the oily grilled cheese sandwiches or the oversalted soup. Grandma sat anxiously looking at the clock. I threw away the leftover food and put the dishes in the dishwasher. The silence and the heat had been unbearable all through lunch. No one had said a single word, though I had very much wanted to ask where the policeman got the idea to come and talk to me. Had Mrs. Johnson said something? But she had no idea what was going on. What if someone had seen me leaving the playground with Julia and Max? What if the policeman already knew everything and was crouching in wait, like a lion, to pounce on me and then calmly devour me?

The doorbell rang. For a few seconds I imagined that the policeman had lost his taste for the hunt and simply come back for me, but then I heard Trudy's voice and breathed a sigh of relief. My grandmother seemed slightly more relaxed, too, as she led Trudy into the kitchen. I could tell the two of them wanted to be alone, so I left and went to the guest room. I needed some quiet time to think things over myself.

The question was, where could Julia and Max go? It was clear to me that the police would soon search the blue house in the barley field, whether they suspected me of anything or not. The kids had to be secretly moved to another location, but I had no idea where, or how to do it. I heard ringing in my ears again, and for several minutes I couldn't hear at all, but it didn't matter. There was no one there who could give me advice or say anything to help me. I lay on my bed for at least half an hour, thinking.

In the end, I had a couple of ideas. The first was that I could only move Julia and Max at night. At night we would have at least a slight chance of not being seen. I didn't really like this solution, though, because I doubted I'd be able to lead them halfway across the neighborhood through the dark without someone seeing us, someone standing at a window peeping out at the end of the day. And that image was horrifying.

The problem was that there wasn't anyplace in or around Clinton to hide them. The police were right there, ready to mess with my plans. But then it occurred to me that there were a couple of places the police *wouldn't* look: the places they had looked *already*. I tried to remember what the people standing out front of the Brandners' house had said, and I came up with the old textile mill. I'd been inside a few times. You could climb in through the broken windows, and then you had to jump down onto a huge field of broken glass. Inside, there was an enormous central hall and a lot of smaller rooms where it would be easy to hide.

The mill. Yes. The mill. My next problem was how to get Julia and Max to come with me. How in the world was I going to convince them to believe my lies? How was I going to get them to wait in the sticky, hot blue house till it was time to go? How could I buy the time? And then I had another idea. It was suddenly just there, and it sent me out into the hall, where my grandmother's cell phone lay charging on the table. It was newer than mine, but it didn't have a password. Then, as I tapped away, I heard voices coming from the kitchen. Grandma and Trudy were still in there, talking.

I bet I knew exactly what they were talking about.

30

The kitchen door was cool against my ear, tickling it lightly. A few seconds ago, I'd heard nothing but whispers. Now the voices were completely clear. Trudy was speaking in her deep, manly voice.

". . . but really, Charlotte, how much do we actually know? There's always an explanation for everything, even Julia's broken arm. Do you remember that?"

"Elsa Levine thought there was something going on. And then her tires were slashed."

"Yes, but that was only because it became clear that the broken arm was just an accident. The girl said so herself."

"I know, Trudy, you're right, I agree. It's just that I sometimes wonder . . ."

"Charlotte! In this neighborhood such a thing couldn't happen. Don't make a drama of it. It's bad blood. After all, what do we know? Nothing!"

"But what about the hamburger at the community

party? Of course, Max is a bit of a glutton, you can see that easily enough. It's got to be hard for Christian and Helen to watch him eat and eat and get fatter and fatter. You've got to ask yourself where it's going to end. But last year at the community party, I remember Christian made him eat a hamburger that was still sizzling hot. He just stuffed it in Max's mouth, and Max went in his pants. You could see the stain on his crotch growing as he stood there. It was so odd how Christian stood around afterward, saying hello to people, being friendly, as if everything was okay. I remember thinking, He can't just have done that. It's simply not possible, what I just saw. It was certainly very strange."

"Charlotte, believe me, what happened that day could mean anything. Anything at all! Things aren't always how they seem. And, just between us, people aren't free to do as they wish anymore. The media would like us to ban everything, even slaps in the face. No one used to care about that kind of thing. But it works, doesn't it. It works."

I wanted to yank open the door and scream. I was so furious. I was thinking, It is possible, it is possible! This whole time, it's been possible!

I thought of Max and how carefully and fearfully he had bitten into his hamburger yesterday. I wanted to scream: *It is too possible!* But I couldn't scream, because I'd promised Julia and Max.

". . . it's really for Helen to do something," Trudy said.

"But she always looks the other way. And if she can't do anything, who can? It's up to her. They're her children, after all."

"She's a miserable creature, Helen. Very weak."

"Although she was the one who got the search going last night. She was driving around all night. Supposedly Christian just stood out front of the house cursing the children. You know: *When I get ahold of them!* Helen's never gone looking for them before. Imagine, those kids staying out the whole night."

"It's unimaginable."

"You should have seen Christian and Helen yesterday morning. They looked different somehow."

"Desperate?"

"Yes, desperate, of course. But something else, too. Determined. Yes, that was it. Determination."

My sweaty ear was stuck to the door, and also my right arm. I carefully peeled them away, but still made the door move. My heart jumped and then was still a second. What if they'd heard me and I was about to be caught doing something else wrong? What could I say, that my ear was itchy and I had been trying to scratch it on the door? Luckily, they went on talking. I wiped my ear on my shoulder and put it back to the door.

"You know," said Trudy. "They recently sued the hospital. Someone at the clinic suspected something, and it turned out not to be true. When I think about what that clinic is going to have to pay. You think twice before you say something in a case like this. And in the end, it's better not to say anything."

"Just like with Elsa?" said my grandmother. "After she came to you, she must have gone to ten different people's doors. And then *she* was sued."

"It was her own fault. Spreading such rumors. It was character assassination, if you ask me, Charlotte. Character assassination and nothing more."

"I'm just saying. They've certainly run away before. Unless—what if Christian just had a bad day?" my grandmother asked.

"That's ridiculous! They've gone to their aunt's."

"Mascha told us something. She saw something through their window. Christian did something to Max. That's all I know."

"She's going to get us all in trouble. All of us, do you understand? The whole community will fall apart. That will be the end of the neighborhood cookouts. And what about us? We'll be stuck in the middle of that miserable situation, even though we have nothing to do with it. Nothing at all."

"Trudy, I know. I don't want anything more to do with this than you do. I told Mascha to keep out of it. Because nothing has actually happened, and none of it really proves anything. And Mascha stopped talking about it. She doesn't seem interested anymore."

"Good girl."

"But it's just, with this situation now. And Officer Price. I almost thought we ought to have said something."

"Okay, Charlotte, let's go over this slowly, once again. Do we have any proof?"

"No! No."

"Do we know anything for sure?"

"N . . . o. We don't know anything. We know nothing at all."

"Good. Let's keep it that way."

31

Let'skeepitthatway.

Let's-keep-it-that-way.

I felt rage, a rage so great it roared in my ears and made my face burn. It rattled my bones and flowed out in my tears.

Then I saw it. Grandma's wallet. Suddenly I had an idea. Maybe not one of my best, but it seemed pretty good at the time. I opened up the wallet quietly, though it probably wasn't necessary to be so careful. In the kitchen, they were going on and on. But I didn't know where my grandfather was; he might be right nearby, and it was also possible that his hearing was sharp enough to hear me undoing the snap.

I looked in the wallet and discovered four bills. After all I'd heard, I didn't think my grandmother deserved that money, but when I had it in my hand, I realized she would quickly realize her wallet was empty. I didn't want to draw her attention. Then I remembered that my grandparents had another stash of money in their bedroom, where they kept their savings for going on vacations.

When I opened the door to their bedroom, I started. There, on the left side of their double bed, lay my grand-father! But when I looked again, I saw it was a pair of pants and a T-shirt laid out as if he were wearing them. Still, my entire body was filled with terror, and it took a while before my breathing went back to normal.

The money. I knew where they kept it. My grand-mother had let me see once, when she ran out of cash. It was in an old candy tin, cherry red with metallic curli-cues and roses on it. *Deluxe selection, 19 pieces.* Forever and ever this old-fashioned tin had sat inside my grand-mother's nightstand, waiting to be opened.

I used my thumb and forefinger to pry off the lid. In-side the tin there was a small stack of bills. The only time I'd ever held such a large amount of money in my hand before was on my birthday, because Dad never knew what to buy me.

But I knew what I could buy for Julia and Max. It was Friday, and the one big department store in town was open late. I had a crisp green bill in my hand. I would buy them so many wonderful things that they wouldn't even notice how uncomfortable it was in the blue house. From the guest bedroom, I took the backpack that I always used for my trips to Clinton, because my suitcase was too small for an entire summer vacation. Then I opened the door, called good-bye over my shoulder and set off.

32

I didn't have to walk through the entire neighborhood to get to the center of town. I just kept to the left, and it was only a few blocks to the next subdivision, but even in that short distance, I saw that there were more people out than usual. On the other side of the street, I watched two old ladies I knew talking excitedly. The feeling of quiet that had always ruled the neighborhood was gone.

There was something in the air. Which made me think of Julia and Max and the terrible smell of the blue house. It must be unbearable by now. I had to hurry if I was going to keep them happy, not to mention convince them to sneak away with me to the mill in the night.

In fifteen minutes, I was at the department store. I cruised through the different sections, buying so many things that I wasn't sure how I'd carry it all back to Julia and Max. By the end, my backpack was bursting at the seams, and I had a hard time closing it.

This is what was in it:

Nail polish
The Big Box of Games (on sale)
A box of blocks
A beading kit
A picnic blanket
Two small pillows (on sale)
A pirate T-shirt (extra large)
A car magazine
A teen fashion magazine
A pad of drawing paper
12 felt-tip pens
Marshmallows
5 enormous chocolate bars
Cotton candy in plastic containers
2 large bags of gummy bears
Paper plates and bowls and plastic utensils
Napkins
3 bags of chips
A bag of salted pretzels
Muffins
3 large bottles of lemonade

With the rest of the money, I went to a fast-food place and bought a large order of fries and two hamburgers. Then, with my jam-packed backpack and bag of food, I headed for the blue house. It was past three, and Julia and Max would be waiting. All in all, I had been gone over two hours. I imagined them banging on the door and cursing me with every bad word they knew. They had no way of understanding how much better it was for them to be in the little house, where no one could hit or shove them.

I decided to pass by the Brandners' house, but the closer I got, the harder my heart began to beat. I was just wondering whether I ought to let myself be seen there with the backpack and plastic bag when I crossed one of the larger streets in town and looked to the left, some fifty yards down the road, to where another large field began.

There were people on the edge of the field.

Men and women, stretched out in a long chain.

Wearing black.

Long sticks in their hands.

Dogs. Dogs on leashes.

Dogs.

They had begun the search.

33

I ran across the street and was nearly hit by a car. It stopped with a squeal of breaks at the very last second, but I ran on with my heavy pack, while the driver shouted at me. At just that moment, the thin handle of the plastic bag gave out, and everything fell with a crash to the ground. I bent down, clutched the bag to my belly and ran on.

Oh, God!

It was so hot.

Not a breath of wind.

But I was shivering.

It was then that I first heard the sound overhead, and to my horror a helicopter flew into sight, red, white and black, moving slowly and carrying the large, dark, threatening letters of the worst word I could imagine through the sky: POLICE. I was sure the men flying in it had already noticed me hurrying through the neighborhood with my backpack, but then the helicopter moved in the other direction.

By this time I was nearly back at my grandparents' house. I turned down a small side road so I wouldn't be seen with the backpack and bag of food. Everywhere people were looking up into the sky and shaking their heads or muttering. The clear skies of the neighborhood had definitely never been polluted by a helicopter before.

I didn't think my legs had the strength or the courage to go another step, but somehow they did. They brought me to the Brandner house and into the crowd of onlookers, all talking wildly and standing around importantly, though not one of them knew anything—not that it seemed to bother them.

I turned, looked across the street and saw Mr. Benrath standing behind his garden fence with excitement in his eyes, waving, and it seemed he was waving at me. The truth is, I wanted to pretend I hadn't seen him, but then it occurred to me that, if he had had a good day, I might learn something from the old man.

"Mr. Benrath, hello!"

"Yes, Mascha, my dear. I have a lovely cup of tea for you, my girl, with real cream."

"But—"

"Come, my dear, let me make you one!"

"You know, I really don't want any tea. I just wanted to ask what's going on. You seem to have a front row seat."

Mr. Benrath smiled and slowly nodded his wrinkled head.

"Yes, yes," he said kindly. "They're gone. It's causing everyone quite a fright." And, then, just like it had done a few weeks ago, the old man's face became serious, taking on a ghostly smile. And in a whisper, Mr. Benrath told me, "Everyone's afraid. Maybe they didn't run away, right? Maybe something really did happen."

"But everybody said they ran away by themselves, Mr. Benrath, even the police."

"Ran away by themselves?"

"That's what everybody said, and the police."

"Ah, but now they don't believe it anymore. No one's seen them anywhere, those children. Certainly not the aunt that everyone was talking about. They got hold of her finally, and she didn't know a thing about the children. So now they don't believe that anymore."

"But what do they believe? What do they believe now?"

Mr. Benrath kept looking at me, and then, after a couple of seconds, for no reason he began to smile happily again. I looked back over at the people standing around in front of the Brandner house and got the impression that this was just another neighborhood party, only minus the burgers, the beer and any reason to celebrate. In the middle of the crowd, I saw Mrs. Johnson, though she, like Mr. Benrath, could just as easily have looked on from her garden fence. She was holding her garden shears and head scarf, talking excitedly with an old man and waving her arms wildly.

She spotted me and called out, "Mascha! Mascha, come over here."

She was trying to lure me with the crooked finger of her right hand, like some witch in a fairy tale. *Forget it, leave me alone*, I thought, and turned quickly away, saying good-bye to Mr. Benrath and taking my backpack, my food and myself away from there.

34

The blue house reeked, and it wasn't just the full bucket in the corner that stank anymore, but the house was also hot and stifling. There was the smell of sweat and the smell of the mattress and the smell of garbage. I looked at the dirty plastic containers from the night before. They stank of rotten food.

It was quiet. Completely quiet.

Here, inside, you couldn't hear helicopters or dogs or Mrs. Johnson. All those things belonged to another world that hardly even seemed real. But Julia and Max? They existed. They were lying on the mattress, right in front of me, but they were completely out of it. Both of them were fast asleep.

Breathing, snoring lightly.

What I saw was horrible, the polar opposite of the happy scene on the mattress the day before. Yesterday everything had seemed all right, almost good, like nothing bad could happen anymore.

But now?

Now the kids looked pathetic.

Julia had damp, sweaty hair and lay rolled up in a ball like before, but this time she seemed weak and defenseless. Her face was an awful color, blotchy gray and red. In her hands she clutched my music player.

Max lay with his legs tangled in my purple leggings, my grandfather's T-shirt pulled up so I could see his belly button as it rose and fell with his breath. His arms were stretched out. His hair was wet and stuck to his head, just like his sister's. His face seemed to glow red against the grandmother-white bedsheet.

For a moment, I just stared at Julia and Max. Then I remembered there were better things I could be doing.

Like airing out the room, now, when no one was going to run away, and emptying the bucket. I grabbed it and went outside, leaving the door of the blue house open at my back. I dumped it in the field and stood there, stock-still. I held my breath and listened. Were they near? Were there dogs barking in the distance? Was that the clattering of the helicopter? But all I could hear was a few birds twittering.

I went back into the house relieved, leaving the door open, and began to unload my backpack, almost in slow motion. First I took out the blue, green and turquoise picnic blanket and spread it on the dusty floor. Then I carefully laid out the things I had bought: the set of games and the magazines and the sweets and then the art supplies and the package of napkins. I folded up Max's T-shirt and put it at the edge of the blanket. I set the nail polish down on Julia's magazine. I unpacked the paper plates and bowls and laid a place at the picnic blanket for each of us. The bottles of lemonade were still cold. I felt glad about that.

The room still smelled from the bucket, but I realized I hadn't really been able to wash it out properly. I went outside, picked some stalks of barley and threw some of them into the damp bucket.

Everything looked beautiful, like a table set for a birthday party. I wished I knew what the table at Julia and Max's birthday parties had looked like. I wondered what you would give to children you spent most of your time hitting and shoving, and whether there would have been gifts. I thought I knew the answer, because it occurred to me that Julia and Max both wore brand-name clothing—at least most of the time, when they didn't have to wear purple leggings from the sale bin. I was fairly sure—certain, in fact—that they didn't have any reason to complain about not getting enough gifts for their birthdays.

Just as I was thinking that, Julia moved and sighed. I jumped up and gently shut the door. But she didn't wake up, and I stood there with no idea what to do with myself. I went to the corner and sat down on the floor. My eyes fell on the picture in the gilded frame. I'd never really looked at the picture before, always focused on the frame, which seemed more beautiful than the painting itself.

The picture was nothing but sea and a tiny boat. Maybe the painter had been out of colors and had nothing but blue to work with. I imagined that if we were in a cartoon, the picture would tip on its side and the water would pour out into the room. I was on the verge of laughing at this when I remembered what was missing here—water—water to drink and water to wash with. As soon as the lemonade was warm, no one would want it anymore, and it couldn't be used to wash with. It would only make everything stickier than before.

How stupid.

How stupid!

I had thought of everything except the most obvious thing. Julia and Max would never even consider my idea of going to the mill because they would be too thirsty and sticky. But no matter how hard I thought about it, no matter how difficult or complicated moving them was going be, I knew they had to leave this place. And they couldn't go home. I'd heard yesterday what their father would do to them if they went back.

Then I remembered my cell phone.

My plan from before.

They wouldn't believe it, they definitely wouldn't, but it was still worth a try.

And just like she was reading my thoughts, Julia finally woke up. She sat up slowly and looked at me with wide-open but still sleepy eyes.

This was my chance.

Before Julia could say anything, I took the phone out of my pocket and said, "Good news! Look what your dad wrote. Your mother's doing better."

It took Julia all of a second and a half to come over to me and read her father's text.

35

Everything ok. My wife better. Will be home soon. –cb

Julia read it aloud three times, never noticing the crucial detail I had stupidly overlooked and was hiding behind my thumb: the telephone number of the sender. I couldn't tell if Julia believed the text or not.

"Everything okay," she repeated, and then she spotted the picnic blanket and let out a small, surprised cry, which woke Max up, too. Julia was stunned and amazed and happy, all at once.

"Mascha. Mascha! What is all that? What is that?"

"It's for you. It's all for you."

"But there's so much. Where did it come from?"

"What do you mean? I bought it. I just bought it."

"But where—where did you get the money?"

"Well, I saved it."

Max rose from the mattress with a yawn, slowly went over to the picnic blanket and kneeled down between the car magazine and the marshmallows. He carefully picked up each of the boxes, bags and packages and turned them in his hands, scratching his head, like someone who didn't understand what was happening. And really, it couldn't have made very much sense to anyone who hadn't been eavesdropping at the kitchen door as Trudy and my grandmother talked.

Max didn't care if it made sense. He grabbed the pirate T-shirt and grunted as he pulled it on over my grandfather's yellow one. Then he began to inspect and unwrap the hamburgers and fries in the plastic shopping bag. Slowly, without any help from us, he divided and arranged the food on the plates. He groaned quietly when a few fries fell onto the picnic blanket but continued with his work. He took several minutes to open the package of napkins, finally poking through the plastic with his finger.

As he wiped the sweat off his face, I thought I saw the beginning of a small smile on his lips. With a great sense of purpose, he folded three napkins into irregular triangles and laid one beside each plate. It looked even more beautiful than before and reminded me even more of a wonderful table set for a birthday party.

Max was so busy with what he was doing he didn't seem to notice us, but once everything was arranged, he looked at me and asked in his rarely used voice, "Why just two?"

Only then did it occur to me that I hadn't been planning to eat with them and hadn't gotten a hamburger for myself. "Don't worry about it, Max," I said. "The fries will be enough for me. I don't really like hamburgers."

We all took our places at the picnic blanket, and I noticed that everything in the blue house felt calmer, more peaceful and almost good. We drank the cold lemonade. Max took a muffin and set it beside his plate. It seemed to taste good to him. Everything seemed to taste good to him. Now and then he would pick up one of the things I had bought, look at it as he chewed his food and then set it back down. Julia, too, kept looking at all the things, and occasionally, in between bites, with her mouth still full, she said, "Man, Mascha!"

36

So that's the way it was.

It was wonderful.

It wasn't a meal like any I ever had. Everything seemed light. The fries were soggy and cold, but they tasted delicious anyway. It might have gone on forever, for years, for decades, till we were old and wrinkled and still we would be eating cold fries.

When the paper plates were empty, we turned to the sweets, stuffing cotton candy in our mouths and following that with marshmallows. Max was eating large chunks of the chocolate, too. His mouth didn't stay empty for more than a second at a time.

Every now and then, one of us would say, "All right, that's it. I'm just going to have one more!" Just one more marshmallow or a few more gummy bears or a little more lemonade. Finally, Max washed down a mouthful of chocolate with too large a gulp of the lemonade and let out a belch so loud that I swear it shook the blue house.

That was how it started. ·

First quietly. Very quietly.

But then we laughed so loud and hard that our eyes ran with tears and we had to hold our bellies. We rolled on the ground at the edge of the picnic blanket surrounded by magazines and chocolate wrappers and laughed and laughed and laughed. We couldn't stop. We laughed so hard it hurt. Julia sat up, laughed some more and grabbed the bottle of nail polish. Color: plum purple. Smell: horrible. She couldn't hold her fingers still because she was laughing so hard, but she didn't care. She painted the edges of her fingers, and every time she looked down at her new plum-purple fingertips, she keeled over in a new fit of laughter.

Max took out the pens and began to color his fingers dark blue, though the color didn't take very well on his nails. He laughed till his face was wet with sweat and tears, gasping in the breaks between laughing.

It felt so good.

The laughter.

Everything.

But since you couldn't live if all you ever did was laugh, and because our laughter slowly made us tired, we laughed more and more quietly, till finally the moment had passed.

Once it was over, Julia opened one of the boxes, and we spent at least an hour playing games. Max took the

paper and the pens and a bag of gummy bears and a bag
of chips over to the mattress and left me and Julia by ourselves with the games and things, including the magazine
I had bought for him.

The two of us sat on the picnic blanket and played
Sorry! But we got tired of it after a while. I saw my music
player sticking out of her pants pocket and I realized how
much I missed listening to my music. I could have used
some Leonard Cohen on all those trips I'd taken back and
forth from the blue house and in all those moments when
someone wanted me to answer a question—pretty much
all the time, over the past day.

I didn't know how to say it, how to ask her. It was
embarrassing somehow. I didn't want to seem like I was
taking back a gift. That's what adults did. But my music
was important to me, and that won out, in the end.

"Julia," I asked. "Do you still need that?"

"What, the music player? Yeah, I definitely need it."

"But Julia. You know. I need the music, too. I get really
depressed when I don't have it."

"I'll give it back to you when we go home."

"I—"

"You know, Mascha, the music, this music, it's really
good. I'm not listening to it that much, because the bat-
tery's almost dead. I'm only listening a little. But this music is something good."

"Yeah, I know. When you listen to it, you can do anything. You know what I mean? When I listen to those songs, my dad is here, and I'm older, and everyone listens to what I say. That's how it is with me."

"And no one can get you, right? When you're listening, no one can get you. Isn't that right, Mascha? The music is around you. It's around me."

"Yeah, me too."

Julia stuffed the music player deeper into her pants pocket and began to open the beading kit. She peeled the tape off the packaging and carefully lifted up the lid. Right then, it seemed like the only thing that mattered to her were the beads. With a slight squint and a curl to her lip, she began to thread them with her plum-colored fingers. I looked over at Max, who was drawing happily away at his picture. I'd hardly noticed him the past half hour, except for the occasional sound of his markers moving across the paper. He seemed to be pleased with what he was drawing. Curious, I went over to him, and peeked over his shoulder at the pad. Everything was—

Everything was brown.

You could see that he had drawn something. A little bit of green showed through and a few blue lines, and some red here and there. But almost everything was hidden behind the brown. There was no way to tell what the picture had looked like, except for the fact that it clearly hadn't been just houses and trees, or he wouldn't have had to obliterate it.

I wanted to ask him what he was doing, but suddenly Julia shouted, "Crap! Crap! Crap!"

When I turned to her I saw that all her beads had come undone. Her face was bright red and she was throwing the beads with all her might at the picture in the gilded frame. And when she got to maybe the forty-ninth bead, she hissed, without looking at me, "Let me tell you something: My father has never in his life said the word *okay*. And he doesn't send text messages. He says texting is for idiots."

37

And then.

And then she screamed.

Without any sort of warning.

She screamed and screamed and screamed, she screamed everything out. "I want to get out of here," she yelled. "I want to get out of here now. Let me out!" She ran around the room like a crazy person, trampling the games and the sweets and the greasy plates. "Mascha!" she screamed. "You stupid cow, you stupid, stupid cow. Why are you keeping us here?" She rattled the door and the grate on the window, but they didn't give, and Julia just got angrier. "We stink, can't you smell it? We're sweaty and filthy and there's no bathroom. Do you realize how horrible this is? What have we ever done to you?"

Although Julia's voice was unbelievably loud, I could clearly hear Max's quiet voice beneath it. He had rolled himself up on the mattress and was stroking his own cheek. He looked like he was trying to soothe himself. I realized he was allowing his imaginary friend, Pablo, to calm him down.

I was standing there looking at this ghostly scene with Max when suddenly Julia reared up and shoved me so hard I fell backward on the picnic blanket. I hadn't expected that, and I began to cry. I tried to stand up, but my hand had fallen on a plate with ketchup all over it, and then Julia shoved me down again.

"Come on, Mascha," she shouted with a fierce look on her face. "Tell us what you think you're doing here."

I mean, Julia was nine. And I was thirteen. She was smaller than I was and thinner. But still I was afraid of her as I lay there on the ground and she stood above me with her terrible rage. More and more tears ran down my face, and I heard her say, "Come on," as if from far away, "it's not true is it, about Mama and how you're supposed to watch us?"

"It is true," I screamed. "You're wrong. It's true." Louder and louder, I screamed, "You're wrong. It's true. You're wrong. It's true. You're right, it's not true."

"What did you just say, Mascha?"

My voice got quieter with my last few words, and I hadn't meant to say what I said. The words just fell out of my mouth and lay beside me on the picnic blanket. I felt so helpless, but I also felt something else: relief. At least I wouldn't have to lie to them anymore. I could save my lies for the grown-ups.

Julia squatted down and asked me again, "What did you just say?"

I had no idea how to explain everything. I couldn't figure out where to start. So I began by standing up from the sticky picnic blanket. Julia didn't help me, but she didn't shove me back down either. She stood up at the same time I did and glared at me with her angry eyes.

"So?" she said.

"So," I said. "So, it's like this."

38

I couldn't stand it anymore, Julia. What they were doing to you. I wanted to stop them."

"They? What do you mean, *they*? Only Daddy does it. And he doesn't really do anything. He doesn't do a thing!"

"But—I've seen it. I've seen your stomach, and I saw when Max landed against the picture frame."

"You're lying again! You haven't seen anything! Nothing at all! Nothing is wrong! We want to go home, we want to go home right now!"

"Julia! You told me about it yourself!"

"I never said anything."

"Someone said your arm—your arm was actually broken once."

"That's not true. Daddy never pushed me off the tree house. He didn't!"

"Tree house? What tree house?"

"He ripped it down."

"But Julia, what about everything you said? This morning you told me—"

"Because Daddy doesn't do anything to us, does he, Max?"

But Max didn't respond. He was not being soothed anymore. I guess Pablo could come and go as he pleased. Instead, Max was sobbing on the mattress. Julia asked him again, "Does he?"

I said, "Julia, if he doesn't do anything to you, then show me your arms and your belly."

She was suddenly terrified. In a panic, she grasped the ends of her long-sleeved shirt tightly between her thumbs and index fingers and yelled, "You'll be sorry if you do anything!"

I could have shouted back at her, but instead I used my normal voice. I thought it would make her understand that I wanted to help her.

"Julia, you can't go back to your house. Your father will beat you. I know. And no one else will help you. Everyone says—"

"Mascha, you promised us you wouldn't—"

"Don't be afraid. I won't say anything. To anyone. But don't you get it? You can't go back to your house! Julia! Don't you get it?"

"You locked us in? You locked us in here? You must be crazy."

"But Julia, I haven't locked you in! It's just—"

"What?"

"Julia, listen . . . Tonight, we've got to get—"

"Tonight? Tonight? You need to let us out of here right now! Max, come on! Stand up!"

When Max didn't move, Julia went over to him and said, "Come on, we're going home!"

He wasn't rolled up in a ball anymore. He was sitting stiffly with his legs stretched out on the mattress, staring straight ahead. Julia reached her hand to her brother, but he stared past it, still sitting. Julia tugged his arm, and he began to strike at her wildly and scream.

She was shouting, "Crap, crap, crap! Why do you have to do this now?"

Then I saw it.

A big wet spot on the sheet.

And while Julia cursed at him and Max continued to hit her, I went to the door and turned around. I knew it was over. But even so, I shouted, "You don't understand anything! I was trying to save you! Don't you get that, you crappy little monsters?" I unlocked the door, slipped through it, slammed it behind me and turned the key.

Outside, just three or four steps away from the blue house, I threw myself in the barley field. I rolled onto my back and stretched out my arms and legs. I must have looked like Max, who had been laying down on the mattress in this same position. Above me, the sky shined a nasty blue. All around me was the gold-gray barley, and my ears rang with the sounds of Julia pounding, throwing herself at the door of the blue house and screaming.

Screaming, "Help!"

Max was screaming, too, but in a different way from Julia. Inside, they raged. Outside, in the field, I lay there, unable to move, not even to do the simplest thing: get up and leave. I lay there like I was dead and everything was done.

They pounded and screamed for at least half an hour, then got quieter until finally there was silence. I stood up, went slowly over to the door and listened. At first I couldn't hear anything, and then I heard something that I could hardly believe.

But it was true.

Julia.

She was finally crying.

39

don't know how I managed to get to my grandparents' house, I really don't know, but somehow my trembling legs carried me back. If a police dog had growled at me or a helicopter had circled over my head, I wouldn't even have noticed.

When I reached their door, I began to feel sick, and at precisely the moment when my grandmother came out of the kitchen and said, "Where are all those cold cuts? And Grandpa's chocolate is missing, too," I threw up all over the freshly washed paving stones and on my grandmother's slippers. It kept coming and coming, new waves of vomit from my mouth. My grandmother asked at least a hundred times, "Mascha, my dear, are you okay? Tell me what's happened."

She didn't make it sound like her clean walkway was more important than me. She was genuinely worried and afraid. "John, come!" she called in alarm, and then she turned back to me and said, "Mascha, you're quite pale.

What is it?" She stood behind me and held my shoulders, which was something she had never done before.

Grandpa was now there holding a bucket, but by then I was only heaving up small amounts. When it didn't seem like anything else would come up, he led me to the bathroom, where I rinsed out my mouth and brushed my teeth. Then my grandfather brought me into the living room and helped me lie down on the sofa.

"Should I turn down the television?" he asked.

"No," I moaned, "leave it." I was happy to be distracted and happy for the tea and the washed-out bucket and my grandmother's care as I lay on the sofa. I still felt sick, and I thought about all the sweets I had stuffed myself with, every single one of them. What I didn't think about was everything else, the things you couldn't eat, that sat so heavily in my stomach.

I dozed. The sofa was soft and smelled a little musty. Sleep, I thought, sleep, just sleep, and then, a hundred years later or maybe just ten minutes, I flinched. *Two children, one seven, the other nine years old, went missing yesterday,* said a voice from the TV. It was hard, but I raised myself up on the sofa and watched the news report. *The children, who are siblings, may still be in the Clinton vicinity, but the police have not ruled out the possibility of a violent crime.*

Possibility.

Possibility.

I let myself fall back on the sofa and listened to the rest of the news and felt like I was deep underwater. I heard, *four foot three and of stocky build*, and then, a few sentences later, *the search will go on until dusk tonight and resume at dawn tomorrow.*

I heard my grandmother's voice. She was standing right beside the sofa, but I couldn't understand her. All I understood was my stomach, which began to churn, and then the vomit surged once again from my mouth and landed on the carpet, right beside the bucket.

40

woke up in the guest room in the middle of the night. Someone must have carried me to bed, probably Grandpa, which was nice to think about. It was too bad I hadn't been awake for it. I still felt awful and could have used more sleep, but it wouldn't come. I lay in bed and waited, waited for something, maybe some Leonard Cohen miracle, maybe to wake up a second time and discover that the whole thing had been a terrible dream.

And then I sat up in bed with a jolt. It was three in the morning and pitch-black outside. I couldn't stay where I was. I just couldn't. My legs were wobbly, my stomach empty and it took me ten minutes before I had my feet on the carpet at the foot of the bed. It took me another ten minutes to dress. It was 3:30 by the time I climbed out the window and set off.

On the path to the barley field.

To the blue house.

It was quiet. Everyone was sleeping peacefully be-hind their blinds. The tidy edges of the lawns were busy growing ragged, making more work for their owners, just to keep them from getting bored. It was cooler than I'd thought it would be. A wind rustled through the dark front yards and across my face.

I decided to take the shortcut again. I wasn't curious about what was happening at the Brandners' anymore. I didn't have any time to lose. I wanted to be near Julia and Max.

The field.

There it was.

Even in the darkness, you could see how perfectly the blue house fit in with the sea of barley. It sat there silently and let the wind pass over its roof. I stood on the edge of the field and listened. I had expected to hear crying or banging on the door. But there was nothing, just this silence, just this wind. I walked through the field and lay down right beside the blue house.

Behind the bars, the window was still open, and af-ter a while I could hear quiet snoring. Definitely Max. I hoped he was more comfortable than I was. Everything about me hurt. The barley straws jabbed me, the earth be-neath was hard and I was chilly because I hadn't thought to bring a jacket. But then it occurred to me that Julia and Max didn't have much more. They were lying on a stinking wet mattress. I only hoped that Max had found my grandfather's pants and put them on.

I lay on my side, with my cheek on my hand. My head was empty. I had no idea why I was there. The wind rustled through the barley, and soon I drifted off and found myself having terrible dreams. I half-woke, then kept falling back to sleep.

Then it was light out, and I woke up for real. I'd heard a noise, but I didn't know what it was.

And then all at once I knew exactly what it was.

It was a dog barking.

I stood up quickly, went to the corner of the blue house and peered around it.

The huge, wide field.

The light breeze.

From far away, I saw them coming.

41

What would happen next at the blue house? I had no idea. I ran as if my life depended on it, ran and ran, stumbling twice, skinning my knees. When I reached the edge of my grandparents' neighborhood, I could see them from far off, standing in front of their door. Grandma was holding something in her hands, something that I only recognized when I got closer.

Max's clothes.

She had found them in the laundry basket.

I started crying. I said, "Oh, Grandma." I wanted to hug her, but she turned away from me and went into the house. My grandfather stayed standing there beside me and laid a hand on my shoulder, but he couldn't look me in the eye.

An hour later, the police came. There were four of them, and they arrived in two cars, which seemed to make an enormous impression on the neighbors. Neighbors crowded along the garden fence and in front of the door. I stood at the kitchen window with pains in my stomach and listened to my grandfather open the door and greet the police. They didn't have to explain themselves. Grandpa knew everything, even though I hadn't said a word for the past hour. Not a word.

Grandma wasn't much better than me when it came to talking. She had locked herself in her bedroom, crying, and wouldn't come out. Though she did say one thing before she disappeared into the bedroom, just one thing, repeated five times, through her tears: "It's all over."

The burden of saying something fell to my grandfather. After all, someone had to talk to the police, and it certainly wasn't going to be me.

Through the window, I watched Trudy standing out in front of the house shaking her head with an angry look on her face, and then my grandfather came into the kitchen with the police, three men and a blond woman. It was the woman who talked to me. I guess they thought a woman would have an easier time getting something out of me. They didn't know I had given Julia and Max my promise, a promise that I would keep forever. It was the least I could do for them.

I sat at the kitchen table and tried to remember what Julia had told me about not being there. She found a spot on the wall and stared at it and imagined that she was somewhere else. I wondered if this was what my father was doing when he stared at the wall. It seemed to work for him; at least he was impossible to reach when he did that.

I looked for my own spot on the kitchen wall and found one: the calendar, which had a recipe for apple butter on it. But it didn't help. I stared and stared but I was still there, my heart pounding as hard as ever, and nothing could protect me from what the policewoman said.

They had found the children in a stinking dump. I nearly said, *Hey, wait a minute, what do you mean* dump? *They were in the blue house.* But it was as if she could read my mind.

"The house was like a dump inside. There were scraps of food, crumpled papers, empty bottles, all these broken toys and the stink—God in heaven, what a stink! What on earth made you lock up those children? They are very upset with you."

—

"A couple more days and— Mascha? Right? Mascha, do you know how hot it can get in a house like that? The children are being interviewed now. Their parents are with them. I think you can imagine what they are saying. Mascha, there must be an explanation. You didn't just lock the children up like that, did you?"

—

"That's what they're saying. They say you put them in the house and locked the door. Is that true?"

—

"Okay, you're not going to talk. Fine. How old are you, twelve, thirteen? Not older at any rate, which is lucky for you, or you could be held responsible. Do you know what that means? Do you know what you've done? Did you ever once think of those children?"

—

"Then let me be clear. This was a kidnapping. Maybe you just did it on a whim, but that's the way the father sees it, and that's the way a lot of people are going to see it. It would help if you would explain yourself."

Suddenly I couldn't stand it anymore. The whole time I had been staring at that hideous calendar and trying not to be there, but it wasn't working. It didn't work. I had been forced to listen to every word. And I just couldn't take it anymore. I jumped out of my chair, and it fell backward with a terrible crash. For a moment I looked at the surprised face of the policewoman. She had a mole on her right cheek, and she had long eyelashes. Then I ran from the kitchen to the guest room and slammed the door behind me.

The police didn't let that worry them. They stayed at least half an hour longer. Grandpa must have talked more than he had in the last two years put together. Then the lock clicked shut, and the house was deadly quiet. I lay on the bed on the verge of tears. I had all the time in the world and was sure no one would disturb me, but still the tears wouldn't come. I couldn't even get sick again. I was empty inside. I lay there on the bed for two or three hours, just staring at the ceiling.

Around noon, I had to go to the bathroom and got up. From the hall, I heard voices in the kitchen and slipped into the tiny guest bathroom that was just beside the front door.

That was when I saw it.

The glass was smashed.

Someone had thrown a stone through the window.

I ran into the kitchen afraid and saw my grandmother kneeling down to sweep up shards of glass. On the floor lay a stone even larger than the one in the guest bathroom. My grandmother was sobbing.

"Your father is coming tomorrow," she said. "He'll take you down a peg."

42

There were no more stones, but we did get a few phone calls, a lisping social worker, the police; and the following day, my father actually showed up. He sat on the garden chair. I didn't want to know what he was thinking because I knew he hated that garden more than any place on earth. He hadn't set foot in it since my mother died. But there he was, unshaven and haggard. It looked like he hadn't eaten for weeks. He was thin and sat there kneading his hands.

It was unbearably hot again that day, with a blue sky. Grandma had halfheartedly baked an apple cake, but it was dry and had no cinnamon. She hadn't looked at me since the day before and still wouldn't, but my father seemed to realize that there was no point treating me like I was invisible or yelling at me. I was miserable enough. He made an effort though. "Couldn't you possibly have done this a little differently?" he asked. "You can't just lock people up. I didn't raise you that way."

Grandpa, who was reading the latest edition of the *Clinton Weekly*, peered around the edge of the newspaper and said in a shaky voice, "Mascha, she had a notion in her head." It was the first thing he'd said about the situation since yesterday morning. I looked at him with amazement, but he was already hiding behind his newspaper again.

I could see the headlines on the front and back pages. On the back page it said things like *Cool Waters Tempt Young and Old* and *Alfred Esser Appointed Chief of Fire Department*. But on the front page it was something else entirely. In great black letters it read *A Child!* And underneath the article there was a photo of the barley field with the house and a few policemen and paramedics and men in white coveralls. The field looked like the wind was blowing through it, but really it was just my grandfather trembling.

Dad said a few more things, but nothing much, and Grandma was still stirring and stirring her coffee when someone yelled something from the other side of the fence. By that time, she'd probably already stirred the coffee cold. A woman stood at the fence, a woman I had never seen before. She shouted "Criminals!" three times. Then she disappeared, and my grandmother began to cry.

"Does anyone ever think about me?" she wanted to know, and did we know that no one would talk to her anymore, and she could just forget going to exercise class, and she might as well drown herself.

"By the time you find a place to drown yourself around here, Charlotte, the whole to-do will be over," Grandpa grumbled back, and I actually came close to laughing.

Grandma pretended she hadn't heard him and then turned to my dad and asked him to take me back home with him, if possible right then, because she couldn't control her granddaughter's behavior.

Grandpa shook his newspaper, and Dad looked pale and said something about my being "old enough" and that "this was bad" but that his film locations were too far away and he only had two weeks left to shoot and that he definitely couldn't take me with him.

"This child!" shouted Grandma, and she was about to go on when Grandpa folded up his newspaper, slapped it down on the table and said loudly, "Mascha will stay here and that's the end of it."

43

So I stayed in Clinton.

And that was the end of it.

For the next few days, I sat in the guest room and did hardly anything but eat my meals and go into the garden. No one talked to me except Grandpa, who tried to be nice and say a few words now and then. The policewoman with the mole came back once. But there was really no point. She couldn't lock me up, and I didn't say a word, not even when she mentioned my mother's death, which had nothing to do with anything. And then there were three letters, all from the same sender: Mr. Brandner's lawyer.

My grandmother barely said a word, except now and then to my grandfather. I was silent, too. I held my tongue from morning to night, longed for my music and somehow passed the days. In the neighborhood, all hell had broken loose, at least according to the newspapers. Grandma was afraid to go out of the house, so she couldn't get them at the newsstand anymore, but my grandfather brought them home when he went shopping.

One afternoon, the newspaper lay open on the kitchen table and I read on page three, in great black letters:

HORROR STORY REMAINS A MYSTERY

FOR FIVE DAYS, a thirteen-year-old accused kidnapper has refused to address the accusations against her. The abducted children, a girl, aged nine, and her seven-year-old brother, are safe with their family and slowly recovering from the ordeal of their captivity. Was this ultimately just a nasty prank committed out of boredom? Police officer Edgar Price remarked, "The children today are increasingly brazen."

Around the area, people remain baffled by the events. According to resident Ramona Silver, "It's scandalous that the girl is not being punished. She might abduct my children next!" Neighbor Rose Johnson is equally apalled: "Everyone here knows the girl lost her mother at an early age, but what right does that give her to kidnap innocent children?" Last Thursday, the girl locked two children in an isolated shack and kept them imprisoned

**there under appalling conditions until Satur-
day. The children were found thanks to a ma-
jor search effort conducted by the police.**

Beneath the article, there were two photos. The first
showed the inside of the blue house and was captioned:
The children were imprisoned in this filthy room for two days.
The second photo was worse. It showed my grandparents,
my father and me in the garden, though you couldn't
make out our faces, and the caption read: *As if nothing
had happened: the young kidnapper and her family enjoying
iced tea in their garden.*

I balled up the newspaper and was about to throw
it at the kitchen wall, but then I thought better of it. I
smoothed it out and shredded it into strips. Even that
didn't help. There was nothing I could do to that newspaper that would make me feel better.

44

You might think that everyone in the whole neighborhood was against us. After all, the place was full of people who were afraid that I would go out and abduct their children next, if I happened to get bored again. There were the broken windows and the shouting woman and the anger on Trudy's face. The strange thing was that there were also people who came to our garden fence and didn't shout. They simply came to talk to my grandfather and sometimes even to lay a hand on his shoulder. I watched from my window, so I couldn't hear what they said, but after their visits, Grandpa always seemed happier, at least a little, and I would have liked to know what they had said to him.

And then just three days before I was leaving, we were sitting in deathly silence eating lunch in the garden. It was noon, and my grandfather was actually reading the newspaper, not just skimming it the way he had the past two weeks. If a reporter had come to the fence and taken a picture of us, the caption would definitely have read: *The young kidnapper and her family enjoying a pleasant luncheon.*

In the middle of this pleasant luncheon, Grandpa said, "George stopped by the fence earlier. He said people in town are talking—"

"Oh, so people are talking, are they?" Grandma said. "Your friend's really got some hot news there!"

But Grandpa didn't let himself get annoyed. He went on calmly, "The doctor who examined the children found multiple injuries. Multiple injuries, you understand. There were too many and they were too old for them to have happened during the abduction, so he called Child Protective Services. Now Christian Brandner is threatening to bring a suit against him for defamation of character. Somehow it got out in the neighborhood and George heard about it."

That was when I stood up. The promise I had made to Julia and Max was suddenly so heavy I couldn't carry it anymore. It was like a suitcase that you have to put down because you just can't bear the load. So I set down my promise and felt an unbelievable anger rise up in me. I began to cry, and I shouted everything out. I told them absolutely everything, even the thing about the elephants and how Max had wanted to die. The beginning of the story my grandparents already knew—what happened with the picture frame, for example—but I told it all over again, all about Pablo, and Julia's belly, and the tree house and the wet things. I showed them on my own body where Max's cuts and bruises were, every one I could remember. I told about Julia and how she tried not to be there. I even admitted how I had stolen the hundred dollars, which made my grandmother gasp, and finally I explained about my promise, and how Mrs. Brandner would die if I told, and the children would be sent to a home. I told my grandparents why I couldn't say anything before, and I cried until I was out of breath. When I finally stopped to breathe, I saw my grandparents sitting there at the garden table with wide-open eyes.

They sat there.

They just sat there and stared at me. My grandmother looked like she wanted to say something, but then she thought better of it and went into the house. Grandpa came over and stood beside me for a few seconds, then hugged me. He smelled like sweat and deodorant, and I didn't know whether I liked it or not—I wasn't used to him hugging me—but I didn't have a chance to decide.

He said, "So, I think this has gone on long enough. I'm going inside to make a phone call."

45

That evening, my grandfather was sitting on my bed, and I didn't even wonder about it because the whole day had been so strange. Strange and depressing, too. My conscience felt better, but I'd still broken my promise to Julia and Max.

Instead of saying good night, I said, "Grandpa, what if Julia and Max are sent to a home, and he really kills their mother?"

My grandfather thought about it and said, "Their mother will be all right, and no matter what happens, the children are alive."

"I don't understand, Grandpa, what do you mean?"

He shrugged his shoulders and said he didn't know for sure but he'd heard that this time Helen Brandner was really going to leave her husband and take her kids with her.

We sat quietly for a while, and then Grandpa said, "What you said about the elephants in Africa, Mascha. Those elephants don't know they're going to die."

"But Julia told me!"

"Yes, it's a legend. That's what people say. But really, the old elephants go into the swamps because their teeth are worn down. In the swamp, there are soft plants that they can chew. And then they die there. In the swamp."

"While they just happen to be there?"

"Yes, you could say that."

"So they have no idea what's going to happen to them, those elephants?"

"No, they just have bad teeth."

It was never really clear how Grandpa knew this, but it wasn't all that surprising to me. In addition to his grass mowing and his grumbling, he read a lot, usually in the evenings, after the local news was over. He grumbled his way through the newspapers, and he grumbled his way through the pages of old books. But they weren't storybooks. They were the other kind of book. Books about real things—like elephants, for example.

After we'd sat there for a few more minutes, I asked, "Grandpa, do you think Grandma will ever talk to me again?"

"Mascha, of course she will! Just give her a little time. For her, for us, this has been a little unusual. And the hundred dollars, she still has to come to terms with that."

"It was stupid, what I did. The whole thing was stupid. It didn't work."

"Let's put it this way. There has probably never been

another child on this earth who has done such a stupid thing."

"Grandpa?"

"Yes?"

"How can you say what you just said so nicely?"

"Well, I guess it's because there has also never been anyone in Clinton who has ever tried to help those children. Except Elsa Levine."

"But Julia and Max hate me!"

"Maybe they do. For now. But imagine how they'll feel when they're older. When they know how things are going to work out for them. And when they remember what happened."

"But—how are things going to work out?"

Grandpa couldn't say. Instead, he told me a little more about Elsa Levine: how no one would believe her back then because fathers who beat their children half to death didn't fit with the whole image of Clinton being peaceful and orderly and fancy. How not even the Brandners' neighbors, who must have heard or seen something, had believed Elsa Levine because Mr. Brandner was the owner of the car dealership, and everyone knew him.

What I didn't understand was why my grandfather hadn't believed her then, since he believed me now. I said that to him, and he thought about it for a long time before he finally spoke.

"Well, I listened too closely to your grandmother. She said we shouldn't mix ourselves up in it. You know, Mascha, I just wanted to be left in peace. I think I wanted what your grandmother did: for nothing to change."

"That's weird. It's so totally boring here. It wouldn't be all that bad, you know. I mean, if something changed around here."

"For you, sure. But for many of us, this is all we have. We don't want any darkness."

"Huh. Grandpa, is there anything that could have been done? I mean, was there any right way to have done something?"

"If only we knew. I think anything anyone did would have been a bit problematic."

"What did the doctor see?"

"Blue bruises everywhere, new ones and old, various cuts. A broken bone that was never set correctly. It must have been awful."

"I know. I saw Max myself."

"It was Julia they were talking about. It was the worst with her."

"Julia? Really?"

"Mascha, I don't believe those children ever lived in a peaceful house. And we were just happy we didn't have to know about it."

"Grandpa! We have to do something."

"I agree. I made a call earlier. Well, we have an appointment for tomorrow."

Then Grandpa explained to me what I could expect to happen the next day, and eventually he said good night, went to the door but turned back one last time.

"Mascha?" he said.

"Yes, Grandpa?"

"They harvested the field. And they tore down the house."

46

When we left the next morning, I felt like a toddler who had just learned to walk. I hadn't been out on the street for two weeks. I set one foot carefully in front of the other. Somehow I had imagined that there would be a thousand people out there, or at least ten, pointing and shouting, but not even Trudy was there. It was just like it had always been.

We could have simply taken a left and then walked in the direction of town, but I asked my grandfather if we could make a detour. I had a large envelope with me that I wanted to leave in front of Julia's door.

Grandpa didn't really like this idea, and I couldn't blame him. I might as well have asked him if we could go to the zoo and take a swim with the crocodiles. Even so, he nodded after a moment. We changed direction and walked side by side through the neighborhood filled with fading hydrangeas, where neither of us was particularly welcome anymore.

The closer we got to the Brandners' house, the more we saw the curtains moving behind the windows of the houses we walked past—people were peering out at us. There were even a few who stood at their fences and shook their heads silently. We saw Mr. Benrath, too, and I wondered how much of the story he knew. He walked up to his fence and nodded at us in a very friendly way, even smiled. It might just have been that he was thinking of all the cream he had in his refrigerator, but suddenly he called out, "John! Mascha!" And then, quietly, he added, "Unbelievable."

"Yes," said my grandfather, and his voice sounded happy and a little surprised.

Mrs. Johnson was in front of her door, just as usual. She flung out her words with an exaggerated smile, "Terrible, just terrible," she said. "What's wrong with the mother of those children? It's no wonder what happened!"

My grandfather grumbled back at her that sometimes nothing's as simple as it seems, and that she ought to know.

We were just a few yards from the Brandners' house. It stood harmlessly across the street, and Grandpa said, "Hurry, Mascha, we have an appointment."

As I was walking up to the Brandners' house, I worried I was doing something idiotic. I had no idea what to do if I saw Mr. Brandner. I bent down in front of the door to lay the package on the step, and that's when exactly the thing happened that I didn't want to happen.

The door opened.

It wasn't Mr. Brandner who came out, though, which was lucky for me, because he would have definitely roared at me and I would have passed out in terror and we would have missed our appointment. No, it was Mrs. Brandner. The door opened so fast, I didn't have time to hide from her or run away, so I just looked at her. At first glance I barely recognized her. She looked almost like new. The purple-yellow blotch on her face was still there, but something was different. She seemed stronger. I could see Julia and Max in her face, the same green eyes with golden flecks. She didn't smile, but she didn't seem angry or upset either.

Then, after we'd looked at each other for a while, she said in a quiet but firm voice, "They told me what happened."

"Here," I said. "This is a charger. It's for Julia."

Mrs. Brandner reached out to take the envelope, and for an instant our hands touched.

Then I heard my grandfather calling, "Mascha, come on!"

I looked at Mrs. Brandner one last time. Grandpa stood there watching me, and I knew that the time had come.

It was time to tell my story.

Acknowledgments

An enormous thank you to Stacey Barney for remembering me and for all your support on this project. Thanks also to Alex, for everything; to Lucy and Willa, for being yourselves; and to the amazing women of my writing space, Powderkeg, where most of the work on translation was done.   —Elizabeth Gaffney